Uncharted

Also by Tracey Garvis Graves

On the Island

Covet

Every Time I Think of You

Cherish (Covet #1.5)

UNCHARTED

An *On the Island* Novella

Tracey Garvis Graves

PUBLISHER'S NOTE

This book is a work of fiction. Names, characters, places, and incidents either are the product of the author's imagination or are used fictitiously, and any resemblance to actual persons, living or dead, business establishments, events, or locales is entirely coincidental.

Cover Design by Sarah Hansen at Okay Creations

For Stacy Elliott Alvarez
and Stefani Blubaugh.
Thank you for believing in me from the beginning.

Chapter 1

Owen

THE HOUSE IS ISOLATED, surrounded by trees and a well-kept lawn. There's a children's play set in one corner of the yard, and an abandoned tricycle on the front sidewalk. Spring has only just arrived in the Midwest, but someone has already drawn a hopscotch pattern with pastel-colored chalk. A sign stuck in the landscaping by the front door announces that the home is protected by ADT, and when I ring the doorbell a dog starts barking, followed by the sound of thundering paws.

The woman that answers the door has a baby in her arms and two toddlers clinging to her skirt. The dog, a large golden retriever, snarls and waits for her to let it out. I hope she doesn't. Her blue eyes narrow as she peers at me behind the safety of a storm door that I'm certain is locked. The glass muffles her voice, but I can still understand her when she says, "Can I help you?" Her guarded tone makes sense, the way it would if you lived out in the country and the world knew your story and had a ballpark idea of your net worth.

"Is your husband around?" I ask.

"He's upstairs. On the phone," she says.

"I'd like to talk to you both. Mind if I wait?"

She doesn't like this. I can tell by the way she pushes the kids behind her and squares her shoulders, lifting her chin

1

slightly.

Ah, she's a fighter. This doesn't surprise me at all.

"You'll have to come back some other time," she says, and starts to close the door. But before she can swing it shut all the way, a dusty pickup truck pulls into the driveway and the relief washes over her face.

The man driving slams on the brakes and gets out of the truck almost before it stops moving. He strides up to me with a suspicious expression on his face. Suspicious and pissed off. I'm older than he is, but he looks enough like me that people could mistake us for brothers; we have the same light brown hair and build.

He glances at the woman in the doorway. "Stay inside." Turning back toward me he says, "Who are you and what do you want?"

"Just wanted to talk to you and your wife."

"Do we know you?"

"No." I put my hands in my pockets and remind myself of the reason for my visit. "My name is Owen Sparks."

The man looks at me, brow furrowed as he filters through his memory for the significance of my name. But the woman, the woman knows immediately, and we both turn toward her when she gasps.

"T.J.," the woman says. She opens the door wide so we can really hear her and the dog shoots out like a bullet from a gun, sniffing me aggressively but thankfully deciding that I'm no threat. "The missing person. The man whose trail went cold in the Maldives. Do you remember? His name was Owen Sparks."

Recognition dawns on his face and they look at me as if I'm a ghost. "Are you the guy who built the shack?" he asks.

"Yes."

"But you're not Bones."

I shake my head. "No." There's no need for me to ask them what they mean. To ask them who Bones is.

Because I know.

They invite me into their home, curiosity overriding their mistrust. I understand their hesitation, but I look harmless enough. I'm wearing jeans and a long-sleeve button-down shirt, purchased a few days ago. My hair is a little long, but it's clean. I even shaved, and that doesn't happen all that often.

Anna holds the door open, shifting the baby to her other hip. When T.J. makes his way across the threshold the two older kids shout, "Daddy!" and jump into his arms, squealing and trying to climb him while he gives each of them a hug. He sets the kids down, leans over, and kisses Anna.

"You okay?" he asks.

She nods and smiles and then he drops another kiss on the baby's head.

I follow behind. "How old are your kids?" I ask.

"The twins will turn two at the end of June," Anna says. "Josie, Mick. Can you say hello?"

My smile falters when she says *Mick*, but thankfully neither of them notices the change in my expression. The kids act shy and don't want to say hello, but they mumble a greeting and then hide behind their parents.

"And this is Piper," Anna adds, ruffling what little hair the baby has. "She's seven months old and crawling everywhere. She'll be walking soon enough and then I'll really have my work cut out for me."

"How did you find us?" T.J. asks, shrugging out of his jacket.

"Internet." It took some searching to come up with their home address, but I'm pretty good at locating people when I put my mind to it. I don't tell them how long I've been offline or that their names popped up immediately when I typed *Maldives* into the Google search box. I was looking for something else entirely, and what I found instead affected me so greatly that it took a week before I was able to read through it all.

And a little longer than that before I could work up the courage to come here.

"Come on in," T.J. says. I follow him from the entryway into the kitchen. "Can I get you something to drink?" he asks.

"No thanks."

"Are you sure?" Anna asks. "We've got Coke, juice, iced tea, beer, bottled water."

"No, really. I'm okay."

"Let me know if you change your mind," she says. The smile she gives me lights up her whole face. She's beautiful in that kind of natural way, and you can't help but notice her eyes, big and blue. I can see why he was so taken with her. She crosses the kitchen to check something that's bubbling on the stove, and I look at my watch. It's almost six thirty. I shouldn't have come so late in the day, so close to dinnertime. They probably have their hands full.

T.J. drops into a chair at the kitchen table and Anna hands him the baby. The kitchen smells good, like garlic bread, and when a timer goes off Anna pulls a pan of it out of the oven. The older kids run in and out of the room, but Anna sidesteps them, and the toys that are scattered around the floor, with ease.

"Slow down, Mick," T.J. says when the little boy crashes into the table. "Are you all right?"

Mick nods, seemingly unfazed.

"Go play with Josie in the living room, okay? Dinner will be ready soon."

"'Kay," he says.

There's a lot of noise and chaos, not unlike the way it is in my village. The place I call home is overrun with kids, most of them barefoot. All of them vying for attention.

T.J. straps the baby into a high chair and drains the pasta while Anna tosses a salad and pulls plates out of the cupboard. They call for the kids to get washed up and T.J. sets the table. They work well together, efficiently and without complaint. My own sister and her husband used to argue about whose turn it was to pick up the phone and order pizza, and I once watched them flip a coin to see who had to change their son's dirty diaper. I haven't seen my sister in years, and while I hate not being a part of my nephew's life, I'm ashamed to admit that I don't really miss her.

"You'll stay for dinner?" Anna asks. I look down and see that they've set an extra place at the table.

"Sure," I say. "That would be great."

During dinner they ask a few basic questions: How did I get to the island? I tell them I found a pilot willing to fly me there. They ask me how long I was there, and I tell them about fifteen months. They want to know how old I am. Thirty-four, I say. I can see by the way they both lean forward in their chairs that they're eager to hear more.

"We'll save the rest of our questions until after the kids go to bed," T.J. says, glancing over at Anna.

She nods.

"Okay," I say. They're so damn nice that it makes me feel even shittier for what I'm going to tell them. I lose my appetite when I think about how they might react, but I keep eating anyway. It's the least I can do.

After dinner, I watch them work together to clear the table and load the dishwasher. I offer to help, so Anna hands me a wet washcloth and points to the kids. I smile and speak to them in low tones as I wipe faces and hands, and the kids don't seem to mind; the baby smiles back and laughs, turning her face away like it's a game.

"You're good with kids," T.J. says. "Do you have any?"

"Not yet." Technically I have a village-full, but none of them are mine, at least not biologically. When I first moved to Kenya I didn't know anything about kids. And it freaked me out a little, the way they looked at me like I'd come to save them. It felt daunting. Now I know that they love anything I do for them, no matter how inconsequential it seems to me. When you have nothing, everything feels like something.

"What's it going to be? *Caillou* or *Dragon Tales*?" T.J. asks the twins.

"*Dragon Tales*," they shout.

"One episode and then it's bedtime, okay?"

"Okay," they say, and then run out of the room.

"I'll turn on the DVR for them," Anna says. She stops in front of T.J. on her way out of the kitchen. "I'm going to lay this one down in her crib. She's about to fall asleep."

The baby smiles, eyes heavy, and T.J. kisses her. "Night night, baby. Sleep tight."

He turns back to me when they leave. "Can I get you a beer? Because I think I could definitely use one."

He doesn't know how true that statement is. I should just tell him to skip the beer and grab a bottle of whatever they keep in their liquor cabinet that's the strongest. "A beer sounds good, actually. Thanks."

"I'll go grab them," he says. "Why don't you sit down in the living room."

I walk down a short hallway and the dog follows me. The twins are lying on the floor in front of the TV, on a big pile of pillows. On the screen a boy and a girl are talking to a pink dragon.

I sit down in an oversize chair and reach down to pet the dog, scratching behind its ears. It flops down at my feet. When T.J. walks back into the room with the beer he says, "Looks like Bo's latched on to you. He's probably thrilled that you haven't tried to ride him."

"He's a good watchdog. He didn't like it when I rang your doorbell."

"We don't get a lot of visitors out here. It's good to know he's still doing his job." T.J. sets a bottle of beer down on the end table next to my chair.

"Thanks," I say.

He sits down on the couch across from me. "I can't believe you're here. We thought…" His voice trails off as he glances toward Mick and Josie. "We thought you were *D-E-A-D*."

I'm hit with an image so visceral that I recoil.

"Hey. Are you okay?" T.J. asks.

"I'm fine." He looks as if he wants to ask me a thousand things but then glances at the kids again and doesn't say anything.

Anna comes back into the room and reminds the kids that it will be time for pajamas and books as soon as the show's over. They protest, but not too loudly.

"Did Piper go down okay?" T.J. asks.

"Out like a light," she answers.

"I opened you a bottle of wine. It's on the counter."

"Ah, I knew there was a reason I married you," she says, leaning down to give him a kiss.

"That's not the only reason," T.J. says, laughing as she walks away. He calls after her. "There were many others, you know."

Anna walks back into the room holding a wineglass. She sits down next to T.J. and takes a sip. "How long will you be in town, Owen?" Anna asks.

"I'm not sure yet," I say. "I'm staying at a hotel in the city." My departure date may be determined by how well this conversation goes. It could be immediate for all I know.

When the credits start to roll on the TV program, Anna picks up the remote control and presses a button to turn off the show. "Bedtime," she says.

"We'll be back," T.J. says. He hands me the remote. "Go ahead and watch something if you want."

I take the remote from him, but I don't turn the TV back on. I wouldn't have a clue about what to watch. Instead I take another drink and look around the room. It's filled with comfortable furniture. There are throw pillows and blankets and a large vase filled with flowers. Family pictures and individual shots of the kids in silver frames are displayed on tabletops and shelves. I can't imagine being on that island for three and a half years, the way they were. No food and water arriving regularly via seaplane. No books or newspapers. No satellite phone. No weekend trips to Malé when they got bored or felt like being around other people. Nothing except for what was already there or what washed ashore. Their home must feel like a safe haven after what they've been through.

I'm still sitting there thinking about what I'm going to say when they walk back into the room fifteen minutes later.

"Can I get you another beer?" T.J. asks.

I start to say no, but then I realize that my bottle is empty. "Okay," I say instead. "Thanks." I haven't had alcohol in a long time, and I can already feel the effect. I'm calmer, though, which is a good thing. T.J. takes the empty bottle into the kitchen and returns with a cold one for both of us. Anna settles on the couch, tucking her legs up under her skirt. She reaches for her wineglass and T.J. sits down next to her.

"I don't even know where to start," I say.

"Start at the very beginning, Owen," Anna says. "Tell us everything."

Chapter 2

Owen

Los Angeles

May 1999

I PARKED MY *BMW* IN the long-term parking ramp at the airport. Professor Donahue would pick it up later, using the extra set of keys I'd given him. "I'm going to drive the hell out of that car while you're gone," he said.

I'd looked at him and laughed. "I hope you do."

I wrestled my large suitcase out of the trunk and pulled it behind me, carrying my duffel bag in my other hand. Trying to strike the right balance of things to bring with me hadn't been easy. In the end I'd decided to be as practical as possible, and my suitcase held mostly clothes and toiletries. Captain Forrester was in charge of buying everything else I would need.

The attractive woman behind the *Emirates* ticket counter smiled at me when it was my turn to check in. She tucked her long hair behind her ears and stood up straighter. Stuck her chest out a little, too. Under different circumstances I might have been interested, but not that day. I handed her my driver's license and passport, watching silently as she tapped on the keyboard.

"How many bags?" she asked.

"Just one," I said.

"The Maldives is a beautiful place," she said. "Have you ever been there?"

"No."

She looked at me and smiled. "Are you traveling for business or pleasure?"

I took the boarding passes she held out to me and my smile was enigmatic at best when I said, "Neither."

My next stop was the locker storage facility near the ticket counters. The short, fat man behind the counter eyed me suspiciously when I pulled a large manila envelope out of my duffel bag. "That's all you want to store?" he asked.

"Yes."

"Contents?"

"Three keys and twenty CDs." The keys were to my car, house, and safe deposit box, and the CDs held information that used to be on my hard drive.

"How long do you want it stored? I can keep it for up to sixty days."

"I want it stored indefinitely."

"I don't do indefinitely."

"Sure you do," I said, smiling politely and pulling a stack of bills from my wallet. I counted off ten one-hundred-dollar bills and laid the money on the counter. Easiest thousand bucks this guy would ever make.

"Okay," he said, just like I knew he would. "Here's the claim ticket."

"I need a pen."

He pulled one from his front pocket and handed it to me. I scribbled out the number on the claim ticket and wrote four numbers in their place, numbers I'd never have trouble remembering. This wasn't the only place I was storing the encrypted data, but if the guy held up his end of the bargain, it would be the easiest place to retrieve it.

"Put this someplace safe. This is the number I'll give you when I come to pick up the envelope."

"Whatever you want," he said as he took the claim ticket

from me. "It's your show."

"Have a nice day," I said, and then I picked up my bag and headed toward my gate.

I landed in Dubai fifteen hours later, eight of which I slept away thanks to the Xanax I'd convinced my doctor to prescribe. *Stress,* I'd said. *I'm not sleeping well.*

Making my way slowly down the aisle, I yawned and stretched and followed the people in front of me into the terminal. I had several hours to kill before my flight to Malé, so I wandered aimlessly through the crowded airport, listening to a jumble of voices having conversations in languages I didn't speak. When I arrived at the departures area in Terminal 1, I stopped at a restaurant serving American food and ordered a burger and a beer. My cell phone remained in my pocket, turned off. I had no desire to see how many messages had piled up. It wasn't like I planned on answering any of them.

With each mile I put behind me, I felt less stress. More confidence in my decision. Maybe it was extreme and completely over-the-top. Eccentric, even. But I really didn't care because all I wanted to do was get lost for a while and this seemed like the best way to do it.

I'd become fascinated with the Maldives after listening to a business acquaintance talk about the chain of islands. "The resorts are amazing," he'd said. "But there are also islands that are completely uninhabited. You can go there if you want. Spend the night, too. They'll come back and get you."

In the days leading up to my company's IPO, when things were really getting out of hand, I couldn't stop thinking about how much easier my life would be if I just walked away from it all. My cell phone I had two cell phones, which rang constantly. So did the one that sat on the big mahogany desk in my corner office. The ringing grated on my nerves and made me feel as if I couldn't breathe. Everyone wanted something from me: time, money, help.

On a particularly stressful afternoon, I picked up the phone and used it to make a few inquiries of my own. Over the next few weeks I obtained a sponsorship visa, which allowed me to enter the Maldives and stay indefinitely. I located a pilot willing to fly me where I needed to go—and purchase the supplies I'd need—with a minimum of questions asked. I expected to hit a roadblock at some point, which would have stopped my plan in its tracks, but I didn't. It's easy to disappear if you have enough money, and I had plenty of it.

And it was in my best interest to be far, far away when everyone discovered that their gravy train had come to a screeching halt.

It was morning when I landed in Malé; I'd been traveling for so many hours that I was already confused about what day it was. I found a restroom and ducked into a stall to change into a pair of shorts and a T-shirt.

The line at the seaplane counter in the arrival hall wasn't long. I waited patiently and when it was my turn I pulled a sheet of paper with a confirmation number on it out of my wallet. "It's a private charter," I said. "Captain Forrester is the pilot."

The woman behind the counter pulled up my reservation on the computer. "You're checked in and ready to go, Mr. Sparks. I'll page Captain Forrester. I believe he's standing by."

"I'm positive he is," I said. I'd paid him generously to be waiting for me, no matter how many travel problems I encountered, or what time I arrived. I knew with absolute certainty that the seaplane would be idling at the dock.

"Please come with me," a uniformed employee of the airline said. I followed him outside and stood at the curb. "The shuttle will transport you to the seaplane terminal. It will arrive momentarily."

"Thank you," I said. Coming out of the air-conditioned building made the heat seem much more oppressive. The air felt heavy and damp when I inhaled, and I started sweating almost immediately. When the minivan arrived I climbed into the air-conditioned interior, telling myself I'd better not get too used to it. After the driver pulled up to the seaplane terminal he led me through a set of double doors. We crossed to another set of doors on the opposite side of the room and then we were back outside. Seaplanes were lined up, tied to a series of rectangular intersecting docks. I handed my boarding pass to the driver and he looked down at it and said, "Right this way, Mr. Sparks."

I followed him to the seaplane and when he motioned for me to hand him my bag I gave it to him and watched as he boarded the plane. Looking around, I took in the blue water and the cloudless sky. Everything seemed so much simpler, and I felt the last of my stress melt away.

A middle-age man popped his head out of the doorway of the plane.

"Captain Forrester?" I asked, stepping forward and reaching out to shake his hand. "I'm Owen Sparks."

He took one look at me and shook his head. "Well, I'll be goddamned," he said, chuckling and clasping my hand in his. "You are not what I was expecting. How old are you, son?"

"Twenty-three," I said. I didn't take his reaction personally; I was used to it. It was the way I conducted business that made me appear older than I was. You couldn't achieve what I'd achieved at such a young age by acting like a punk. People treated me with respect, listened to what I had to say.

I had no doubt that my net worth also set me apart from most of my peers. And there were times—like right then—when I was glad I had so much money. I'd earned it, and it was nice to use it for something I really wanted instead of feeling as if I had to give it to everyone just because they had their hand out.

"Well, come on," he said. I followed him through the door of the cabin, and he pointed to the rows of seats behind him. "Sit wherever you like. Just make sure to fasten your seat belt."

My duffel bag had been placed on a seat in the front row, so I sat down next to it and stowed it on the floor at my feet. I watched as Captain Forrester placed a headset on his head and started flipping switches. He spoke briefly into the microphone near his mouth, and as soon as he had clearance, we pulled away from the platform. We picked up speed and I felt the thrust when we lifted off.

As we flew I looked out my window, amazed at the view. I

squinted against the bright sunlight that flooded the cabin and dug my sunglasses out of my bag. The cloudless sky was just as blue as the water below.

It took close to two hours to reach our destination. I hadn't seen any land in a while, but finally the plane descended and I got my first look at the island. It wasn't overly large, maybe a half mile in length. Pristine, white-sand beach. Green vegetation. Palm and coconut trees reaching high up to the sky in the densely forested area near the center of the land mass.

I remember thinking that nothing bad could ever happen in such a beautiful place.

We landed right in the lagoon.

"Better take off those shoes," he said.

I smiled when I looked down at his feet and realized he'd been flying the seaplane barefoot.

After I took off my shoes and shoved them into my bag he swung open the cabin door and we jumped into the knee-deep water. He opened the cargo hold on the side of the plane and we started carrying my supplies to the shore, making several trips in order to unload it all. Small schools of fish darted away as I walked in water as warm as a bath.

"Let's go through the checklist and make sure I didn't miss anything," he said, after we'd placed the last of the gear on the sand. From his shirt pocket he pulled out a folded piece of paper that I recognized as one of the emails I'd sent to him.

The first item was an Iridium satellite phone. "My number is already programmed into it, so if you get in trouble, or you need me, all you have to do is push this button," he said, pointing to it and handing the phone to me. He leaned in and pointed to another button. "If for some reason I don't answer, call this number. It's the airport. The battery should last for months if you don't start calling people when you get lonely."

"I'm not going to call anybody," I said. There wasn't a single person I'd left behind that I wanted to talk to.

He reached for the next item, a large backpack resting on the sand. It was the kind that serious hikers used when they wanted to go backcountry camping and not be dependent on anyone else to carry in their supplies. The last time I'd used a backpack like this was when I was twelve years old. For my birthday I'd asked my dad to sign me up for a week-long backpacking and rock-climbing expedition in the Sierra Nevada mountains through Outward Bound. My dad and I loved to camp, and he'd been taking me with him for as long as I could remember. My mom wasn't interested and neither was my sister, but I never felt happier than when I was outdoors, and the more remote the location, the better. When my dad brought the Outward Bound brochure home and we read through it together, I knew right away that I was up for the challenge.

The seven days I spent in the wilderness was everything I had hoped for, and it changed me in ways I didn't fully understand at the time. But my dad died of a brain aneurysm two days after I got back from my Outward Bound expedition, and I hadn't been camping since.

Now, standing on the beach, I wondered if my desire to live on the island, alone and in such a desolate place, was my attempt to re-create the way I felt on that expedition. I was too young back then to experience a true epiphany, but I'd sensed that something larger existed. Some sort of awakening that could be achieved only by living in a place virtually untouched by other humans, in total solitude.

I unzipped the backpack and pulled out the contents: sleeping bag, ground mat, and tent. I didn't necessarily need the backpack, but it kept everything contained and made it easier to transport the items from the seaplane to the beach. It might come in handy when I explored the island.

He picked up the list and made a checkmark as I sifted through the contents of a large cardboard box and said them out loud. "Camp stove, fuel, knife, lighter, flashlight, fishing pole, tackle box, a pot and pan, first-aid kit, utensils, insect repellant, sunscreen, solar shower, shovel, a large, wide-mouth plastic container, toilet paper, and garbage bags."

The nonperishable food was next. Everything was dehydrated and vacuum-packed or in a can with a metal pull tab. There were plenty of nuts, dried cereal and fruit, beef jerky, and a powdered drink mix I could add water to. Cans of green beans and corn. "The lagoon is full of fish. There's coconuts and breadfruit. You'll have plenty to eat."

He pointed to the three seven-gallon containers that contained drinking water. "Keep those in the shade," he said. "The water won't be cold, but it'll stay a bit fresher. It's not enough to last you for thirty days, but if you collect rain water in this—he held up the plastic container—you'll be fine."

"Okay," I said. Making sure I had enough water made me nervous. When I first started corresponding with him, and explained what I wanted to do, he said that lack of fresh water was the biggest obstacle to living on an uninhabited island.

"Make sure you put everything that can't be burned in one of the garbage bags. You'll bring it back with you so we can dispose of it."

I planned on treating the island as I would a campground, respecting it the way I would any piece of land I was temporarily inhabiting. "I won't leave any garbage behind."

One of the first questions I'd asked was whether it was even possible to do what I wanted to do—and would he agree to help me do it?

"Most people visit these uninhabited islands for a day or two, max," he'd said. "They have a picnic and get their *Robinson Crusoe* fix, and then they're ready to head back to their resort. I've never known anyone who wanted to squat on one of them indefinitely. But if this is what you really want to do, I know of a place that might work. It's far out on the northern edge and there isn't any air traffic to speak of. The risk of a seaplane landing in the lagoon with a couple of honeymooners on board is nil, so I don't think you'll have to worry about anyone discovering you."

"That's exactly what I want," I'd said.

When everything was unpacked I looked over at him, took a deep breath, and said, "You must think I'm crazy."

"I'm not gonna lie, son. That thought has crossed my mind. Either that or you want to get away from it all more than anyone I've ever known."

I had my own reservations. This was easily the most self-indulgent thing I'd ever done. "Maybe I'll get it out of my system quicker than I planned on," I said.

He wiped the sweat from his face with the tail of his shirt. "Now listen, from now until about November is when you'll see the most rain. You shouldn't have any trouble collecting water to drink because it'll rain several times a day. Just make sure you always have your container ready. Dehydration is your biggest threat here, so be very aware of your water supply."

I knew the Maldives had two seasons—the rainy season, or southwest monsoon, which was the season we were currently in, and the drier northeast monsoon, which would begin its changeover in December. "What about the storms?" I asked. "How severe are they?"

"They're not like hurricanes—those occur only in the Western Hemisphere—but some of the storms could be pretty strong."

"Will I be able to ride one out in my tent?"

"You should be able to," he said, nodding his head. "I'll watch the radar, listen to the weather reports. If I think there's one brewing that's too much for you to handle, I'll come get you." He laid a hand on my shoulder. "You've got to be careful here, son. Use caution in the water and on the land. This island isn't like one of the resorts." He squeezed my shoulder and dropped his hand.

I found it amazing that this man I didn't even know gave a shit about my welfare, considering my own family didn't seem to care about anything other than *theirs*. It made me feel good, like for once the weight of the world wasn't just on my shoulders. "I'll be okay," I said. "But I appreciate your concern. Thank you for everything."

He smiled and extended his hand. "You're welcome. Call me if you need me. Otherwise, I'll be back in thirty days."

"Okay."

We shook hands and I watched him walk away, the tails of his extra-large shirt flapping in the breeze. He waded into the water and the sound of the seaplane engines soon filled the silence.

When he was nothing more than a speck in the sky I turned around and started living my new life.

Chapter 3

Owen

Journal entry

May 15, 1999

I ARRIVED ON THE ISLAND today. I set up camp on the beach and in the late afternoon, without warning, it started pouring rain, which was kind of weird because the sun was still shining. The heat is stifling. When I wasn't in the water I stayed in the shade, but the bugs were horrible. I sprayed myself from head to toe with insect repellant. It didn't keep all of them away, but most. I noticed a couple of the biggest, creepiest spiders I'd ever seen. They're brown with really long legs, and if I ever find one of them in my tent I will probably scream like a fucking girl.

When the sun went down the bats came out. It was one of the most incredible things I've ever seen. There were so many of them that when they filled the sky they blocked the light of the moon.

It's quiet here, nothing but the sound of the waves. Most people would probably hate it, but I've never felt calmer or more at peace.

May 17, 1999

I spend most of the daylight hours exploring. There are schools of fish in the lagoon, and I wish I had a snorkel so I could see them better. I've spotted crabs and sea turtles and yesterday I thought I saw a fin, but it dipped below the surface of the water before I could get a good look at it. I got out of the water, just in case.

I forgot to ask about sharks. I know they're here, but I don't know if they come inside the lagoon.

I should probably find out.

May 21, 1999

I don't know how or why, but there are chickens here. I was walking in the most densely forested part of the island yesterday, where the sunlight only reaches the ground in narrow beams, and I heard this weird flapping sound. Then a chicken flew straight up in front of me, and I almost shit myself. It ran away like it was afraid I might chase after it, which was hilarious considering I was frozen in my tracks waiting for my aorta to explode because my heart was beating so fast. I swear it took five minutes before all bodily functions returned to normal.

May 24, 1999

Questions:
Chickens. What the hell?
Is there anything in the lagoon that can kill me?
Giant brown spiders—poisonous?
It didn't take long before I settled into a routine of sorts. I woke up early and every morning I went for a swim and then made coffee on my camp stove. After a breakfast of cereal and dried fruit I usually wrote in my journal and then explored another part of the island.

It no longer felt so hot, and there were times when I stretched out on the sand, protected by an SPF of 50, and let the sun beat right down on me. When I did get too warm I got in the water or found some shade. I'd brought my favorite book with me, a dog-eared paperback of Stephen King's *The*

Stand. I'd open to a random page and see how Frannie and Stu and Glen and Larry were dealing with the superflu.

Strangely, I wasn't bored. There was always something to do or see, and by the time I'd been on the island for two weeks, I'd covered almost every inch of it. I'd come across a chicken several times—maybe it was the same one—and it always took off flapping when it heard me coming. I also discovered that the island had an incredibly large rat population, but they mostly came out at night, their eyes glowing in the dark as they scuttled along the ground.

I'd spotted the fin in the lagoon again, but this time there were two. Shielding my eyes with my hand, I stood on the shore and squinted. They didn't look like sharks, but I wasn't sure. I waded in a few feet, keeping a careful eye on the fins, but got out of the water quick when they disappeared below the surface.

I started trying to guess the time of day by looking at the sun's position in the sky. Several times throughout the morning and afternoon I'd make a guess and then pull my watch out of my pocket to see if I was right.

It rained frequently, which was good for my water supply, but so far it hadn't stormed. One day the sky grew dark and I sat in my tent and listened as the rain came down in torrential sheets, but the sky cleared after an hour and I breathed a sigh of relief.

I started thinking about whether it would be possible to build some kind of fixed structure on the island, something sturdier in case the weather ever really got bad. The idea took hold and I opened to a blank page in my journal and made a few sketches. As a kid, I'd been obsessed with Legos and Lincoln Logs, spending hours building elaborate structures. I'd always wanted a tree house, but my yard didn't have the right kind of trees to support anything that big. I liked the idea of building something on a large scale, with my own two hands. Something that I could use for shelter.

Something that felt a bit more like a home.

Chapter 4

Owen

Journal entry

June 4, 1999

THE SEAPLANE WILL RETURN IN eleven days. I'm not lonely—not really—but it will be nice to hear another human voice and have a conversation with someone.

I've discovered I like fishing. Using various lures that I found in the tackle box, I stand waist-deep in the lagoon, waiting for something to bite down on my hook. I've caught fish ranging in size from six to twelve inches, but I only catch what I'm able to eat at my next meal. The first time I had to clean a fish I made a holy freaking mess out of it and almost sliced my finger open with the knife. I'm getting better. It's been a long time since I went fishing and my dad was always the one who cleaned them, so I'm learning as I go.

I found out that the fins I kept seeing in the lagoon belong to dolphins and not sharks. Three of them swam close to shore one day and I felt relieved when I saw their bodies break the surface. I've been slowly easing myself into the water when they appear and they're starting to swim closer to me. There are usually two or three of them and the other day one blew water out of its blowhole. Like it was saying, hi Owen!

I've been swimming for increasingly longer periods of time. I swim parallel to the shore, in water that isn't too deep, and I don't stop until my shoulders and chest ache and I'm too out of breath to continue. I feel amazing afterward.

June 7, 1999

The dolphins are fascinating. It took a while, but they're finally starting to trust me. I caught some small fish and threw one into the mouth of the dolphin that swam the closest, and now he? she? isn't scared of me at all. I talk to them and it's like they understand what I'm saying.

June 10, 1999

I spent over an hour hand-feeding the dolphins today. I don't think I've ever used the word "frolic" in my life, but that's the only thing that describes what I see when the dolphins show up and start swimming alongside me and leaping into the air. They turn onto their backs and let me rub their stomachs and they don't mind at all when I grab on to their fins and hitch a ride around the lagoon. I've started thinking of them as my friends.

I hope that doesn't mean that I've started to lose my mind or anything.

The seaplane arrives tomorrow.

Chapter 4A

Anna

IT'S SO HARD TO WRAP my brain around what Owen is telling us. As I listen to him describe his early days I can't help but remember T.J.'s and mine. I remember thinking that since I was the adult it was up to me to figure it all out, and the knowledge of that—the fear—nearly crushed me because I had no *idea*, no clue what to do. All I knew was that I was terrified and certain that we would die.

Glancing over at T.J., I pause. The man sitting next to me on this couch is my equal, my confidante. The love of my life. He is strong in every sense of the word. But I think back and remember him at sixteen: skinny, unsure of his role, braces on his teeth. Scared. In my mind I can see T.J.'s cracked lips, the cuts on his face, the eye that was swollen shut. Thrust into another life-or-death situation that he had no choice but to face head on and fight.

If we hadn't been in such a dire situation, would we have appreciated the beauty of the island the way that Owen had? Could we have felt the peace that he felt? It doesn't matter, because we can't compare our time on the island with Owen's.

Eventually, we did acknowledge the beauty there, just like Owen did. But we never once forgot how vulnerable, how powerless we were. For us there was no seaplane dropping off supplies. No satellite phone. Nothing that tied us to the outside world. No one to help us. The only thing that was true, the one constant during our time on the island, the thing we could depend on, was each other.

I look over at T.J. He shows no emotion on his face, and I'm not sure what he's thinking. Is he remembering how different our first few weeks were? I reach over and grab his hand because right now at this moment I need to *feel* our connection. When he squeezes my hand I squeeze back, the way I always do.

And then I turn my attention back to Owen, because as hard as it is to deal with these memories, I want to listen to what he has come here to say.

Chapter 5

Owen

I WAS WAITING ON THE beach when the seaplane landed in the lagoon. Relief flooded through me when I heard the sound of the engines and spotted the plane in the sky. Though I was getting closer to it every day, I hadn't been on the island long enough to become one hundred percent comfortable with cutting ties to the outside world. I still needed to know that a connection to it existed. That it was there for me, and I could count on it if I needed it.

I'd stuffed my dirty clothes into my duffel bag and battened down the rest. I stored everything inside the tent and made sure to drive the stakes as far down into the sand as I could so the whole thing wouldn't blow away if it stormed. I was planning on spending only one night on the mainland and would return early the next morning once my supplies were loaded on the plane. I put all the garbage I couldn't burn into a plastic garbage bag and I hoisted it over my shoulder.

Barefoot, I waded out to meet Captain Forrester. I hadn't bothered with a shirt, but he didn't seem the type to mind. I tossed my duffel and the garbage bag in first, and he smiled at me when I hauled myself through the cabin door.

"Wow," he said. "That's one hell of an impressive suntan." He reached out to shake my hand and clap me on the back.

"How're you doing, son?"

"I'm doing great," I said, returning the smile. "It's nice to see you again."

"I'll be honest, I half expected you to call me after the first week to ask me to come and get you. I wouldn't have blamed you if you'd lost your shit a little. Glad to see you handled the solitude well."

"Yeah. Solitude was exactly what I was after."

"I think you found it. You can sit up front if you'd like," he said, once he'd shut the door and settled himself back into his seat.

"Okay." I sat down in the seat beside his and fastened my seat belt.

"So, tell me what you've been up to," he said once we'd taken off. "You ready to pack it in and go home for good?"

"Not yet," I said. "I kinda have a routine. Met some dolphins."

" I've always thought that animals make the best company. As long as you don't pose a threat to them, they'll keep coming around."

"Yeah. It's awesome, actually. It's like they understand what I'm saying."

"I wouldn't be surprised if they do," he said. "How are the supplies holding up?"

"I'm low on water. I drink more than I thought I would because it's so hot. Food's okay, though. I've been fishing a lot."

"Nothin' tastes better than fish you catch yourself. Too bad I prefer mine deep-fried and covered in tartar sauce," he said, laughing.

I laughed. "Yeah. Me, too. But they still taste pretty good the way I cook them."

"Have you tried the coconuts?"

"Yes. They're not easy to get into. I almost sliced my hand open the first time I tried."

"The coconuts make you work for their meat, there's no doubt about it."

"Did you know there are wild chickens on the island?"

"Yep. Most islands have a few running around."

"Do you know if the spiders are poisonous? The big brown ones?"

"Those are brown huntsman. They're creepy looking, but harmless."

"What about sharks?

"The whale shark is the most common, but they pose no threat. There are hammerheads here, which could do some damage, I guess. Reef sharks for sure, but they don't usually bother anyone. I imagine most of the sharks will stay on the other side of the reef, so the lagoon should be safe," he said. "But it's not like there's anything keeping them out if they decide they want to come in, so be careful."

"Do you think it'd be possible for me to build something on the island? Out of wood? I could use it for shelter when it storms."

"Depends on how big you'd want it to be," he said.

"Not too big," I said. "I don't really know what I'm doing, so I'd have to learn as I go. Could supplies like lumber be flown in? Would there be room on the plane?"

"Sure, there's room. I might not be able to bring it all at once, but I could bring enough to get you started," he said. "It's not a bad idea if you think you're going to stay for a while. It'll keep you busy, at least."

"I do," I said. "I definitely think I'll be there for a while."

After we landed I pulled my shirt and shoes out of my bag. The shoes felt weird; I rarely wore them unless I was in the wooded area of the island. I pulled my T-shirt over my head and followed Captain Forrester through the cabin door.

"Do you have your list of supplies?" he asked.

"Yes." I reached into my pocket and handed him the list I'd made. "Did the wire come through okay?" I asked.

"Yes. It came through just fine. I'll buy everything on your list and have it waiting for you on the plane."

"Okay," I said. "Thanks."

"Sure," he said, and smiled.

"I'll be ready to go by nine tomorrow morning, if that still works for you."

"Works fine," he said. "Enjoy your evening."

He'd booked me a room under his name at the Hulhule Island Hotel near the airport. I caught a shuttle bus and in less than five minutes I was standing in front of the check-in desk. The woman who assisted me smiled and handed me a key card.

"Enjoy your stay," she said.

"I will. Thank you."

When I reached my room I threw my bag on the bed and immediately turned off the air conditioner. I opened the window to let in the heat, which I now preferred over the cool air.

In the bathroom, I had to take a closer look when I caught the first glimpse of my reflection in the mirror. My skin had never been so dark before. Even though I lived in sunny California, I'd been ghostly pale when I arrived on the island, due to sitting in front of a computer for twelve to fifteen hours a day. My major source of light had been the fluorescent bulbs in my office.

A month's worth of facial hair covered my face. I'd packed a disposable razor and a can of shaving cream, and could have shaved if I'd wanted, but it didn't seem that important, so I'd skipped it. My hair had grown too, but it was so short to begin with that I could probably hold off on the haircut until next month.

I stripped off my clothes and took a long hot shower. It felt strange to return to such modern conveniences after my time on the island. Everything seemed so attainable, as if there wasn't anything I couldn't have if I wanted it. I almost felt guilty although I had no idea why.

When I was done showering I dried myself and then wrapped the towel around my waist while I shaved. The hotel offered laundry services, so I gathered up all my dirty clothes and called the front desk. They promised to send someone up for them right away, so I put on the robe I found in the closet and stretched out on the bed.

I thought about plugging in my cell phone, but I really didn't feel like checking to see who had called. If my family and friends looked through my old journal—the one I'd left in plain sight on the nightstand in my apartment—they'd know of my intent to come here. If they were that concerned about my well-being, and not just my money, they'd know where to find me.

The sad thing was that I really didn't think they'd bother to make the effort.

I ordered lunch from room service and then took a nap while I waited for my laundry to be returned. A knock on the door roused me from sleep and when I opened it a hotel employee handed me my clothes. They smelled a lot better than they did when I arrived. "Thank you," I said, and I gave her a generous tip.

After I pulled on a T-shirt and shorts I slid my feet into my tennis shoes, grabbed my key card and my wallet, and walked to the lobby. I took the shuttle back to the airport and then boarded a ferry called a *dhoni* for the short trip to Malé. It was painted in shades of bright blue and orange and filled to capacity with tourists.

Once I arrived on the mainland I decided to walk to my destination. I could have rented a motorbike or taken a taxi, but I wanted to see the capital city. The tourist brochure in my hotel room said that almost anywhere in Malé was reachable on foot within ten minutes.

I made my way through the city streets, stopping to browse at the local market, watching as the locals mingled with the tourists. Clusters of bright yellow bananas hung overhead, and merchants stood next to tables selling local produce and fresh fruit.

I encountered the fish market a couple of blocks away; I smelled it before I saw it. A bustling crowd made up of fisherman and customers filled the area, and I stopped and watched the men cutting fish, their slicing way more precise than anything I was capable of. I'd gotten a lot better, though, and now

I wasted almost none of the fish when I cleaned them.

I spied a sign that said NOVELTY BOOKSHOP. That was the main reason I'd taken this side trip to Malé. After crossing the street I pushed open the door and stepped into the air-conditioned space. Shelves of stationery and office supplies lined the walls. There were rows and rows of novels and text-books, and I walked past them slowly, reading the titles on the spines, searching. The air smelled slightly musty, the way it always did when so many books were stored closely together, but it was a familiar smell and reminded me of all the time I spent in the library in college.

I finally found what I was looking for in the nonfiction section, near the self-help books. The selection was limited, but there were several books on house framing. I picked up one and opened it to the table of contents. There were chapters on the materials and tools I'd need, and also the various building techniques. I stood there for fifteen minutes flipping through the books, finally choosing the one that had the most infor-mation on everything I'd need to know. I added all the current issues of every business magazine they sold, and that day's edi-tion of *USA Today*. I didn't regret my decision to leave the business world, not for a minute, but I still felt the desire to know how the current trends were playing out.

When I left the bookstore I was whistling because I never felt better than when I had a plan.

That night I ate dinner at the bar in my hotel. I sat outside on the deck and ordered a beer and a cheeseburger and fries, which tasted better than any burger and fries ever had. I or-dered another beer after my plate had been cleared and drank it while watching the sun set over the Indian Ocean. When it was fully dark the lights of Malé lit up the sky.

I wandered inside and took a seat at the bar. Many of the customers were playing pool or throwing darts. They seemed to be a mix of businessmen wearing suits and seaplane pilots wearing short-sleeve shirts bearing their airlines' names and logos. There was a definite shortage of women, which bummed me out because after thirty days alone, I would have been more than happy to spot a girl sitting at the bar.

I had one more beer and then I called it a night and headed to my room. Before I went to sleep I opened the house-framing book and made a long and detailed list of everything I would need.

The next morning I showered and ordered coffee and breakfast from room service. I needed to be at the dock in fifteen minutes, so I crammed my purchases from the bookstore into my bag and checked out.

Captain Forrester was waiting for me. "Good morning," he said. "Ready to go?"

"Yep." I followed him through the cabin door and once again buckled myself into the seat next to his and watched as he went through his preflight routine.

"I made a few calls," he said. "I can get the lumber you wanted. The man I spoke with said they'll cut it for you. Can you give me a list of what you want? Probably won't be until next week, though. That okay?"

"Sure." I fished a piece of paper out of the pocket of my shorts. "Here's a list of everything I'll need. Just send the invoice to my email address. You should receive a wire payment within twenty-four hours."

He looked at me strangely and said, "Exactly what kind of business are you in, son?"

"Dot-com," I said, answering him quickly. For some reason—maybe because he'd been so helpful and so nice—it was important to me that he didn't think I'd earned my money by dealing drugs or from some other sketchy activity. "But I'm not in the business anymore. I sold my interest in the company right before I came here."

"So you had partners?"

"I had three." Scott and I had grown up together; he'd moved into the house across the street from mine when we were in first grade. I'd met Tim and Andrew my freshman year at UCLA. The four of us formed an online company after graduation, to sell advertising space over the Internet. We registered our domain name and took advantage of low interest rates and market confidence. Everyone we knew was scrambling to come up with the next big thing and we were every bit as eager to join the Internet gold rush.

"It must have been a pretty successful company."

"We did okay," I said.

The company hadn't been my first online venture. I'd already had great success selling things on eBay, before the auction site really hit the mainstream. One of the first things I sold was my sister's old Barbie doll collection. I offered her a sixty-forty split and sold the whole lot for five hundred dollars. It had been so easy—nothing more than a few mouse clicks—and after that I was hooked.

I spent my weekends combing newspaper ads and driving to estate sales, buying up anything I thought I could sell for a profit. I didn't have enough room in my dorm, so I carted it all back to my mom's house and stored it in my old bedroom or the garage or anyplace else I could find to put it. My mom had remarried three years after my dad died—to some deadbeat I hadn't liked or trusted since day one—and my piles of inventory drove him nuts. I told him I'd pay their mortgage if he stopped complaining, and since he was frequently unemployed he wisely agreed. He shut up after that.

I couldn't believe how much money I made during my senior year of college. Most months I earned in excess of twenty thousand dollars, and the only reason I didn't earn more was because there were only twenty-four hours in a day. I had always done well in school , but I had to pull frequent all-nighters in order to balance my business demands with my course load and assignments.

After I graduated with my business degree I decided that I wanted to expand, to do something on a bigger scale. Something that didn't require collecting and storing such a large amount of inventory. Selling online advertising space seemed like the perfect solution, and I joined forces with Scott, Tim, and Andrew, who were equally enthusiastic. That was the first mistake I made.

Like many start-ups, we spent ninety percent of our fifteen-hour workdays that first year trying to generate publicity for the company. Publicity for a company that had yet to produce anything. We went after venture capital aggressively, and investors couldn't wait to give it to us. They didn't seem to mind taking a risk on us, and why wouldn't they? We were four confident, well-educated rising stars with a slick business plan. It didn't hurt that a national business publication had dubbed us "four to watch."

We'd poured a lot of our seed money into our office space and it was Scott's idea for us never to be seen in anything other than suits and ties, even on the weekends. I hated that, and protested loudly, but I was outvoted, and suddenly we were all dressing like bankers.

The nice cars and the expense-account lunches and dinners came next. I hated those, too. I wanted to be in front of my computer working. Creating. Not telling everyone how great we were going to be. Once again I was outvoted, and I bought a BMW and parked my truck in my mom's garage.

To me, it all seemed like smoke and mirrors. We started having a lot of heated disagreements, and finally I asked them to buy me out. We'd raised a staggering amount of business capital by then, and I asked for three million dollars. In exchange, I'd sign away my right to any future profits. They thought I was crazy, and Scott even pulled me aside and tried to talk me out of it; I think he felt guilty. But I had a bad feeling about the direction of the company and just wanted out. I had plenty in the bank already, and three million on top of it meant I could go anywhere and do anything I wanted.

Captain Forrester's voice interrupted my thoughts. "Do these former partners of yours know where you are?" he asked.

"No," I said, because I hadn't bothered to tell them. I didn't know if I'd ever see those guys again. Not even Scott, my childhood friend. He'd been the one to change the most, and it was his urging that usually resulted in the riskiest business decisions. He had big goals, but I highly doubted his ability to execute them.

"Sounds like the company was doing pretty well," he said.

"Any regrets?"

Sometimes I thought about the millions I'd walked away from. A local newspaper had done a story on us, and they'd listed everything in detail: our salaries, assets, projected earnings. We looked like we had money to burn. It didn't help that they took pictures of our offices and one of Scott standing next to his Range Rover. Suddenly, everyone knew our business. And it was funny how people changed when they found out you had money. How they acted like you owed them some of it and didn't deserve to keep it all simply because there was so much. My sister had been the first to ask. She said if it wasn't for her letting me sell her Barbie dolls, I would never have been successful. It was bullshit, and we both knew it, but I gave her the money anyway, thinking it would be a one-time request. That was the second mistake I made.

"No. No regrets at all," I said.

When we reached the island we carried the fresh supplies to the beach, mostly food and water and fuel for the stove. I smiled when I opened a box that contained canned goods and toiletries and noticed the snorkel mask and fins tucked in next to them. "Hey," I said. "I meant to ask you for these. You must have read my mind."

"I figured you could put them to good use. There's some of the best snorkeling in the world here."

I couldn't remember the last time someone had done something thoughtful for me, and I felt oddly choked up. "Yeah. This is great."

He looked around at the boxes and said, "Well. That's all of it. I'll be back in about a week with your lumber and tools. I'll bring what I can and fly in the rest as you need it."

"Thank you," I said. "I really appreciate all you've done for me."

He smiled and said, "You're welcome, son."

We shook hands and after he lifted off I watched him until he was no more than a speck in the sky.

Chapter 6

Owen

Journal entry

June 18, 1999

I'VE SPENT MOST OF THE last two days snorkeling in the lagoon, stopping only when the dolphins joined me. Everything looks so clear when I view it through the mask. The colors of the fish are brighter and I can see things I couldn't see before, like their stripes or other markings. I've ventured out to the reef a few times. The water color gets steadily darker, and once it's no longer light blue I know I'm in deep, open water. It makes me nervous because I remember the warning about sharks.

I read the first five chapters of the house framing book I bought in Malé and made a few sketches. I'm anxious to get started. Tomorrow I'm going to pick a spot to build.

June 19, 1999

I can't wait until I have my building supplies because I found a great spot in the woods. It's not too far from my camp on the beach, and the trees should give me some extra protection from the storms, as long as none of them fall on my house. I'll have to clear the surrounding vegetation, which will be backbreaking work, but I've already used the shovel to dig up some of the undergrowth.

June 20, 1999

I saw a shark today. I went snorkeling after lunch and spent over an hour near the reef. I was so mesmerized by everything I saw that I didn't notice the shark until it swam right up beside me. I think it was a reef shark. It took everything I had not to panic.

I jumped when the satellite phone rang. The only reason I heard it at all was because I'd reached inside the tent to grab a shirt out of my duffel bag when the call came through. I wasn't used to hearing the sound of a phone—I wasn't used to hearing any sound other than the crashing of the waves—and it took a second for me to figure out what was happening. I managed to find the phone, buried beneath my clothes, and grabbed it before he hung up. The display read FORRESTER.

"Hello," I said.

"Oh, good. It works," he replied.

"Uh, did you think it might not?" I asked.

"The guy who sold it to me said it can be a bit temperamental."

"Oh. Okay. I'll keep that in mind." It didn't really bother me that the phone might not always work. The trips back to the mainland were my safety net. Even if something happened—if I got sick or injured—I knew the seaplane would return, eventually. I switched the bulky phone to my other ear. "What's up?"

"The pressure's dropping. There'll be a storm tonight. Nothing severe, nothing you can't handle. Just didn't want you to stress out and think I'd left you there to ride it out on your own. You'll get a lot of rain. Some wind. Nothing too terrible, though."

"Thanks for letting me know."

"No problem. Your lumber and tools will be ready tomorrow. I'll fly it over in the morning."

"Did the wire come through okay?" I hoped my voice didn't sound as anxious to him as it did to me.

"Your wires always come through just fine," he said. "No

need to worry. I'll see you tomorrow. Take care tonight."

"Thanks. I will,"

That evening, shortly before the sun went down, the winds picked up and the water churned in the lagoon. Lightning streaked across the sky and I could almost feel the drop in barometric pressure. I waited nervously, and when the full brunt of the storm arrived I watched the nylon sides of my tent ripple and strain at the seams, but luckily everything held and after several hours the storm died down. It was the worst night I'd had since coming to the island because I felt vulnerable and completely at the mercy of the elements.

Maybe by the time the next one rolled in I'd be well on my way to building something better equipped to withstand whatever Mother Nature had in store for me.

I was sitting on the beach eating breakfast when I heard the drone of the engines. When the seaplane landed in the lagoon I waded out to it and we spent the next half hour unloading all the building materials from the cargo hold. Once we'd carried everything to shore he asked, "How, exactly, are you going to build this house by yourself?"

"Slowly, and with a lot of trial and error," I said. "I bought a book. That should help a little, I hope."

"Just how long are you planning on staying here? I'll be honest, I didn't think you'd make it this long. But you seem to like it here," he said, chuckling. "So now I'm curious."

"I don't know. Is there a problem if I stay? My visa is open-ended. Do you think anyone would care that I'm still here?"

"Well, I suppose they'd have to find you first. Most seaplanes take a more direct route on their way to the resorts. Anyone flying in this vicinity would need a reason for being so far out on the northern rim. So if they did come across you, then they'd still have to decide you were worth stopping for. Most pilots probably wouldn't take a second look, to be honest. It's not that unusual for tourists to visit the uninhabited islands. They just don't stay as long as you have. Unless you were standing on the beach with a roaring signal fire and a giant *SOS* drawn in the sand, a pilot probably wouldn't bother to investigate."

I nodded my head. "Okay."

"You didn't answer my question," he said.

"I guess I'll stay here until I have a good enough reason to go someplace else."

Chapter 7

Owen

IT WASN'T EASY BUILDING A house by myself. I stopped frequently to consult the book that lay open at all times, sometimes literally scratching my head as I tried to figure out what to do next. I didn't have anyone to hold the boards steady, so I had to rig a system using tree stumps propped up beside the framed sections to hold them in place. I lost track of how many minor injuries they inflicted when one of them hit me in the head or fell on my foot.

It was tedious and laborious, but that didn't really bother me. While I worked I let my mind wander, and sometimes, when I pulled my watch out of my pocket, I couldn't believe how much time had passed. I'd never done anything that physical before, and my muscles ached in new places every day. One day I was so sore I could hardly lift my arms over my head when I took a break to go swimming. But the muscle soreness soon faded, and I made slow and steady progress.

As the weeks went by I spent more and more time in the woods. I no longer noticed the mosquitoes, the spiders, and the heat. Often I'd work until it was fully dark and the rats came out, but even they didn't bother me too much.

I remember being amazed the first time I realized that I'd somehow turned the pile of lumber I'd carried into the woods one board at a time into something that sort of looked like a house.

In mid-October, I picked up the satellite phone and pressed the button that said FORRESTER. When he answered the first thing he said was, "Is everything okay?"

"Yeah," I answered. "Everything is fine. Great, actually. I just wanted to tell you that I don't want to visit the mainland this month. I was hoping I could give you my list over the phone and you could bring everything to me. Maybe stay for an hour or so."

"Sure," he said. "Tell me what you need."

"I need more lumber for sure. I'm low on nails and screws, too. Oh, and wood glue. I should have been using that from the start. As for everything else, just bring the same things you've been bringing. Maybe a little more food. I've been really hungry lately."

"Okay," he said. "Lumber and food. I can do that."

"Thanks. See you soon."

When the seaplane landed in the lagoon a few days later, I could hardly contain my excitement. It wasn't because I had a visitor—not really—because by then being alone felt natural. Sure, I took comfort in knowing that being on the island for five months hadn't turned me into some weird recluse or anything. I still had the desire for companionship and conversation. But I wanted to show someone what I'd built with my own two hands. I felt proud of what I'd accomplished so far, although by all accounts the wooden structure was hardly that impressive. But it was the first time I created something that was tangible. That I could see in all its dimensions. Walk around the perimeter. Step inside and be surrounded by four real walls.

I waded out to the plane. He shook my hand and clapped me on the back. "Should have told me to bring some scissors, son," he said, laughing. "Looks like you could use a haircut."

I'd skipped the haircut the last time I spent the night on the mainland. I had every intention of visiting the barber but then decided I'd rather spend the afternoon drinking in the hotel bar with some tourists from Germany. My attempt to keep up with them resulted in me passing out in my hotel room and sleeping through until early the next morning. When I awoke with a pounding head I swore I'd never drink again.

I ran my hands through my shaggy hair. I'd picked up a small mirror in the hotel gift shop, and I'd been making more of an effort to shave, but I had at least a week's worth of stubble on my face. "Yeah, I'm not all that well-groomed these days."

"Eh, who gives a shit," he said.

"Obviously, not me," I said, laughing. "Did the wire…"

"… Come through okay? Yes. It came through just fine," he said. "Come on. Let's get this stuff unloaded. I want to see what you've been doing since I was here last."

When everything was once again stacked on the beach I led the way toward the center of the island. I turned around and watched his face when we reached the house. His eyes grew wide, and I could tell that what I'd done had surpassed his expectations. He walked in a circle around the entire house. "I can't believe you did this all by yourself," he said. "I'm really impressed."

"It was pretty slow going at first, but I'm getting faster. Framing it was the hardest part. I put it together in sections on the ground, but I didn't have anyone to help me lift them into place. I figured it out, though."

"You've done a great job," he said, using his forearm to wipe sweat from his face. "You built your very own fortress in the woods."

"Well, fort anyway," I said, laughing.

"I don't think men ever quite outgrow their desire for one."

"No. I guess they don't."

I decided to fish for our dinner. It didn't take long to catch and clean three decent-size fish, and soon they were sizzling in the frying pan. "Can I help you with anything?" he asked, lowering his large frame to the ground near the camp stove.

"No thanks. I've got it." Noticing that he didn't look all that comfortable I said, "Maybe I should have asked you to bring some lawn chairs. Sorry about that."

"It's okay," he said. "I've just got about thirty years on you. My joints aren't as forgiving as they used to be."

I filled a small pan with water and when it came to a boil I opened a small plastic pouch and poured in some dehydrated scalloped potatoes. When the fish were done cooking I removed them from the pan, pulled the tab on a can of green beans, and dumped them in, adding a bit of water. By the time the potatoes finished cooking, the beans would be heated through.

"It sure is peaceful here," he said. "I'm used to the resorts, and all the people bustling around. The noise."

"I've gotten used to it," I said. "I like not hearing any sound other than the waves."

I stirred the potatoes, took them off the heat, and put the lid on them. The beans were simmering so I turned off the stove and made our plates, handing one to him. "Thanks," he said.

I sat down beside him and we ate. "Have you talked to your family lately?" he asked.

I shook my head. "I haven't talked to them since I left home."

"That must have been some falling-out you had."

"No falling-out. They just don't really care." I sounded like a spoiled teenager when I said that, and he picked right up on it.

"I'm sure they do care."

I set down my plate and wiped my mouth with the back of my hand; napkins had never quite made it onto my supply list. "In March of 1999 my company donated money to purchase refurbished computers for a public school in a lower-income district. We received requests for donations all the time, but no one wanted to grant this one. My business partners said it wasn't high-profile enough. I lobbied hard for it, though, and they finally agreed, probably because they got tired of hearing me talk about it."

He set down his empty plate.

"Do you want some more?" I asked. "There's still some left."

"No thanks," he said. "Go on."

"The principal and the teachers at the school were beyond appreciative and wanted the presentation of the check to be part of a school-wide assembly. I arranged to have a reporter and a photographer there when we presented the check. I figured the kids would get a kick out of seeing their picture in the paper and it would get my partners off my back because it would generate a little publicity.

"Because my mom was the one who bought me my first computer I thought she and my stepdad might want to come. I was proud of what our company had done. I hoped maybe the donation would inspire another kid to get interested in computers the way I had been at that age. I left a message on my mom's answering machine, giving her the details about when and where the assembly would be held, but I didn't hear back from her. She and my stepdad traveled a lot, so I wasn't sure she'd even get the message. I'd been working really long hours and it had been a while since I'd seen her." I hesitated for a second, because I wasn't sure I wanted to tell him the rest, but for some reason I found it easy to talk to him. "I don't care for my stepdad. He married my mom about three years after my dad died, and we've never really gotten along.

"Anyway, I didn't hear back from my mom, but on the day of the school assembly I spotted her and my stepdad in the bleachers. I felt really good, you know?"

He nodded.

"When the crowd thinned out and the students started heading back to their classrooms, I walked over to them. I finally felt like I had done something worthwhile and seeing them there made it even better. I should have known that something was up, though. My stepdad wasn't smiling and my mom just looked worried. Turns out they were heading to the airport, to catch their flight to Hawaii. But there was a problem with the money I wired them every month. The problem was that it hadn't come through."

"You wired them money every month?"

I nodded. "My stepdad hadn't worked in two years. He couldn't find a job that was a good fit, he said. I'd already been paying their mortgage, but he pulled me aside and said it might be better if I just transferred a set amount into their joint account each month and they'd take over paying the mortgage and the other bills. 'Better for you,' I said to him. I didn't want to do it, but I worried about my mom. She was a customer-service manager, and she worked hard. I found out from my sister that my mom had been picking up extra shifts. If money was still tight for them, even without a mortgage to pay, it made me wonder what my stepdad had been spending it on. I hated the thought of her putting in extra hours and still not being able to get by, so I said I'd do it, even though the monthly amount he suggested was ridiculous.

"It was the first day of the month and I don't know what happened, but the automatic transfer I'd set up didn't go through. It had always worked before, so my mom and stepdad stood there in that empty gym and waited while I called the bank. Apparently there had been some sort of glitch and they fixed it over the phone.

"Ah," he said. "Now I understand why you always ask."

"My stepdad walked away but my mom stayed behind. She thanked me for the money and told me she was proud of what my company had done for the school, and proud of me. She hugged me and when she pulled away she had tears in her eyes. Then she said good-bye and hurried to catch up with my stepdad."

"I'm sorry."

"They hadn't come to the assembly for me at all. It was only for themselves and the money. That's all I really was to them—a source of income. People will keep taking as long as you keep giving. It was the same with my sister. At first everyone for was grateful for the gifts. Then they started to expect them. Then they seemed to be angry I wasn't giving them even more. Like they deserved it and resented me for even having to ask. A few days before I left California I canceled the automatic wire transfers. I paid off the mortgage so my mom would always have a roof over her head."

"Does she know you're here?" he asked.

"Yes. But she's the only one who knows. It would have made me feel like shit to worry her. I met her after work shortly before I came here and told her about my plans. I said that I was leaving my journal behind and if anyone wanted to, they'd be able to trace me to the Maldives. After that, I knew they probably wouldn't be able to find me. I told her that the money I used to wire every month would now go into an account with only her name and mine on it, and it would be there if she ever wanted to leave her husband. It requires two signatures for a withdrawal, hers and a man named Brian Donahue, who's one of my professors from college. He was the only person I could trust. I called the bank from my hotel room on our last supply run. So far there haven't been any withdrawals, so she's still choosing him, which is fine. Love over money, right?"

"That's the way it should be," he said.

"But if she ever wants to leave, she can." My sister—who had never stopped asking for money—got one final lump sum, and I did not feel the least bit guilty about cutting her off. It was large enough that if she blew through it all she'd have no one to blame but herself. She'd married about as well as my mom had, and I would have loved to see the look on her husband's face when he realized there wouldn't be any more money.

"What you've done is very admirable," he said. "But don't you feel like you're the one missing out? You're the one who had to walk away from everything."

I shrugged. "Maybe. This feels like enough, though. At least for now."

Chapter 8

Owen

I FOUND THE CAVE IN January. Strangely, in the eight months I'd been on the island I'd never noticed it. I happened to be looking down when I walked by, and the pile of sticks and rotting leaves that had blown up against the opening caught my eye.

I cleared them away and cautiously stuck my hand in, trying to feel around. I walked back to the beach and returned with a flashlight, then crawled forward enough to poke my head all the way in. It smelled musty and I realized just how small the space was. I had to wedge the flashlight under my arm and wriggle through on my stomach. The area wasn't much larger than my two-person tent. There wasn't anything interesting inside, just more leaves. Something scurried slowly across the floor, but when I pointed my flashlight at it, it darted away. I shone the light onto the roof of the cave, hoping I wouldn't see hundreds of bats hanging upside down. Fortunately, there wasn't anything above me other than a few of those giant brown spiders that I still hadn't gotten used to. I was lucky there weren't any bats, because if the cave was where they hung out, I probably would have crawled right into a big pile of their shit.

I backed out of the cave and stood up, taking deep breaths

to clear the musty smell from my nose. *No reason to go back in there,* I thought.

No reason at all.

For the next four months I focused on finishing the house. I'd never call myself a great carpenter, but as the house took shape I felt like I'd done a pretty good job, considering my lack of training. The house had two rooms, with a door between them. The hardwood floor felt too rough to walk on with bare feet, so I spent hours sanding it by hand, wearing out sheet after sheet of sandpaper. I had to thatch the roof because I wanted to save my lumber supply for the walls and floor, but I'd had enough to build a framework of wooden beams, which I then covered with intersecting layers of palm fronds. I moved all my belongings inside the house, and I tried sleeping in it for a few nights, but I preferred my tent on the beach and the sound of the crashing waves. The sounds were much different at night when I slept in the house. There was a constant drone from the bugs and a scurrying sound from the rats. Lots and lots of rats. It wasn't horrible, but I still liked the ocean sounds better.

It was the dry season and the weather had been mild, so I didn't know how well the house would stand up to a storm. Because it didn't rain as much, I depended on the water that was flown in more than I had in previous months. And every thirty days or so when I heard the seaplane's engines, I smiled because it meant I'd have company for dinner.

When I wasn't working on the house I was in the water, swimming laps. I had no doubt that I was in the best shape of my life. I could swim for a long time without getting winded, and I felt stronger than I ever had. I knew I'd gained weight, and that it was pure muscle.

When I wasn't swimming laps I was snorkeling. I'd finally grown comfortable in the open water. There was so much to see that sometimes, when I ventured into the deeper depths of the ocean, out where the light blue water turned dark, I forgot about just how low on the food chain I really was. It was on one of those days that I experienced a truly incredible encounter, although when I first caught a glimpse of it out of the corner of my eye I froze in terror, certain that I would be swallowed whole by this massive creature.

I realized suddenly that it was a whale shark, frighteningly large but not interested in eating anything other than plankton. It must have been forty or fifty feet in length, and I swam next to it, one hand on its side. It glided through the water, its mouth open until it turned and swam away. I watched it go, certain that I'd just seen something that not many people ever would.

In May, just before the rainy season began again, I decided I wanted to visit the mainland. I really needed a haircut; I didn't mind wearing my hair long, but it had gotten to the point where it was constantly in my eyes and made the back of my neck sweat. Plus I'd been craving a cheeseburger and a beer, and I felt like taking a real shower and sleeping in a bed for a change.

And for the first time in a year I started to think that maybe it was time to figure out what I wanted to do next.

After I checked in to my hotel room I got my hair cut and then stopped at the hardware store to stock up on nails and screws in case I needed to make any repairs to the house. I wandered the streets of Malé for a while, just people watching. I could tell the locals from the tourists and the tourists from the expats with ease by then, just by what they were wearing. The locals were partial to T-shirts with business logos while the tourists wore bright surf wear or clothing with the logo of their resort. The expats seemed to always be dressed in worn and faded clothing, and the ones I'd struck up a conversation with had usually traveled extensively throughout Asia.

I made my way back to the hotel so I could drop off my stuff before heading down to the bar on the main level. I sat inside instead of at my usual table on the deck because it was raining. The weather suited my mood, indifferent and slightly depressed. I told myself to snap out of it.

"Hello, Owen." The waitress, a local woman who looked about my mom's age, set a menu and a bottle of beer down in front of me.

I smiled at her. "Hi, Donna."

"I haven't seen you in a while," she said. "I almost didn't recognize you with that short hair. Where've you been hiding?"

"Oh, you know. Just hanging out on the island." I never said which island, and Donna never asked.

"Burger and fries?" she asked.

"You got it," I said. "Thanks."

She scooped up the menu and said, "Coming right up."

After I finished eating I pushed my plate away. When Donna took it I relocated to an empty stool at the bar, hoping a few more drinks would put me in a better frame of mind. The place was packed that night, and I'd been lucky to snag a seat. One of the seaplane pilots I'd met a few months back walked by.

"Up for a game of pool?" he asked.

"Maybe in a little while," I said. I didn't feel like playing; I didn't feel like doing much of anything at all. Maybe now that the house was done I needed a new goal, something to work toward, to occupy my time and my mind. I wasn't sure if the island could provide that any more. Equally frustrating was the fact that I wasn't sure exactly what I was looking for. But whatever I decided, I needed to figure it out soon.

I took a drink of my beer and looked around. A girl sitting at the end of the bar caught my eye. I couldn't hear what she was saying, but she was laughing and gesturing wildly with her hands, whipping her head back and forth as if she was telling a story to the people sitting on either side of her. I couldn't remember the last time I'd come across anyone who seemed so genuinely happy.

When was the last time *I'd* been happy like that?

I watched her out of the corner of my eye and noticed the way she paid special attention to the blond guy to her right. How she rested her hand on his shoulder and shoved him. She must have been joking, though, because she smiled at him and he smiled back. I looked down at my drink. For a minute I felt lonely and it was the kind of loneliness that had nothing to do with spending my days and nights on an island by myself.

Two beers later, I had a nice buzz going and felt a little better. But it was getting late and I thought it might be better to stop while I was ahead. Get a good night's sleep and shake off the remainder of this funk I was in. Hope that the sun would be shining when I woke up. I was about to close out my tab when the girl from the end of the bar slid onto the newly vacated seat next to me.

"Hi," she said. "Is anyone sitting here? Bit crowded where I'm at. Can't seem to flag down the bartender."

She had an English accent, which took me by surprise, and she looked close to my age, maybe a little younger. It was hard to tell with girls sometimes. Her cheeks were slightly sunburned, her eyes were green, and her blond hair was pulled back in a ponytail.

"No," I said. "Go ahead." Her glass was almost empty. "Can I buy you a drink?"

"Sure. I should probably stop after this one, though," she said, laughing. "I'm half-pissed already."

I signaled the bartender to bring us another round. "I'm Owen."

"Calia." She reached out and shook my hand.

"Nice to meet you," I said. "Where are you from?"

"Surrey," she said. "A small town called Farnham. Been here on holiday for two weeks visiting a friend who works at one of the resorts. Fabulous time. What about you?"

"California."

"Just arriving or heading home?"

I shook my head. "Neither. I'm staying on one of the islands. I came back to the mainland to get some supplies."

She looked at me strangely. "Why do you need supplies? The resort should have everything you need."

"I'm not actually staying at a resort. My island is a bit less... inhabited."

Her eyes grew wide. "Is it completely uninhabited? I've heard you can visit those islands. They'll pack a picnic lunch for you and everything."

I laughed. "Well, it's been a bit longer than a day trip for me."

"How long?"

"About a year."

"You've been living on one of those islands for a *year*? By yourself? Voluntarily?"

Great. When she said it like that it made me sound like some kind of fruit loop. "Yeah," I said. "I felt like taking a break, getting away from it all." I shrugged.

"Wow," she said.

I didn't know if she would understand that there was something about the remote location that spoke to me. That I had my reasons for the solitude. And I was suddenly aware of the fact that I did *not* want this girl to think I was weird. "I wanted to challenge myself. See if I could do it."

She looked at me and smiled. "Well, I think it's incredible."

"Really?" I asked. My mood was improving by the second.

"Yes." She leaned in and lowered her voice to a conspiratorial whisper. "Is that why you visit the bar while you're here? To pick up a girl along with your supplies?"

She seemed so genuinely curious, and so serious, that I shook my head and laughed. "No," I said. "I'm not usually lucky enough to find a girl here." *Especially one that's so pretty.* "So thanks for giving me something other than these men to look at," I said.

I could smell her perfume, and sitting so close to her at the crowded bar, our arms almost touching, stirred up all kinds of things in me. I might have sworn off most people in general, but I'd been thinking a lot lately about how I missed women in particular.

"You're welcome," she said. She smiled, and I couldn't be sure but I thought I noticed a slight flush on her cheeks. "I know it's not quite as bold as living on an island alone, but I'm moving to Kenya in the fall."

"Why Africa?" I asked.

"I'm going to join a volunteer mission. I want to experience new things, but I also want to help people. I just graduated from university, but I don't want to be stuck behind some desk. I mean, what's the point?" The more she talked, the more passionate she became. Her voice got a little louder, a little more determined. She looked me in the eye and said, "Did you know that over one million children have been orphaned by AIDS in Kenya?"

"No," I said. "I didn't know that."

"It's true. And often kids as young as ten have to leave school to find a job so they can support their younger siblings." She shook her head. "It's tragic. There are so many people who need help. If I can make a difference in just one person's life, it will be worth it. Especially if that person is a child."

I admired her fervent desire to help people, unlike me and my desire to hide from them. "I think what you're planning to do is very commendable," I said. "Where will you live?"

"Another volunteer and I are teamed up. We'll stay in a communal area in the village."

"Is that safe?"

"The volunteer coordinators have assured us that it is," she said. "I'll be fine."

"When do you leave to go home?" I asked.

"I'm flying out tomorrow, actually."

"Oh," I said, nodding. Of course. Why else would she be in the airport hotel bar? "You must be ready to get back home."

She shrugged. "I have the whole summer ahead of me. Not sure what I'm going to do with all the time, actually. I could get a job, but it would have to be temporary since I'll be leaving again in three months."

I realized as she spoke that I could sort of see down the front of her dress. Not a lot, but enough to remind me just how long it had been since I'd slept with a girl. That had been the last thing on my mind when I left California, but it seemed to be the first thing on my mind every morning when I woke up. And several times throughout the day. And again at night.

Maybe that's why I said, "Come with me."

"To your island?"

"Yeah. Why not?"

She didn't miss a beat. "Maybe I will."

I figured she was just blowing smoke, and she probably

turned that killer smile on lots of guys. "Sure," I said, laughing. "I'll believe that when I see it." She wasn't particularly rugged looking. In fact, she was kind of slight. Delicate almost. Frankly, I couldn't picture her on the island or in Africa or anyplace even remotely primitive.

She laughed and said, "You shouldn't make assumptions. My life is temporarily lacking in adventure."

"So it's adventure you're after?" I asked.

"Among other things," she said.

What is that supposed to mean? Jesus, I really was out of practice. What if I'd completely lost the ability to determine when a girl was interested in me? I'd feel stupid if I took her seriously and she was just kidding. I decided to call her bluff and see if she confessed that there was no way in hell she planned to join me on some remote island. "You know there's no bathroom, right?"

Her forehead creased with worry, but just for a second. "No bathroom, you say?"

"No, so don't say I didn't warn you. I've got a solar shower—which isn't bad, actually—but there's no running water. No electricity. No modern conveniences of any kind."

"If I was bothered by those things, I wouldn't be going to Africa now, would I?"

"Good point. Okay, then. Consider yourself officially invited. Come for a visit and stay as long as you'd like. I've got a satellite phone and a pilot on call who can bring you back to Malé at any time. Meet me at the seaplane dock tomorrow morning at nine."

"I'll be there, Owen."

"Well, either way, it was nice meeting you."

I paid my tab and headed back to my room. Before I went to bed I picked up the phone. When the voice mail beeped I said, "I invited this girl to come to the island with me. She probably won't show. I mean, that would be crazy, right? But just in case, I was wondering if you could bring some extra supplies." I paused, realizing how stupid I sounded. He'd probably look at me with pity tomorrow morning when he saw me standing on the dock by myself like a big loser. "On second thought, never mind. She's not gonna show, so don't worry about the supplies. Well, maybe you should. No, never mind. Okay, bye." I hung up the phone.

There was no way this girl was going to meet me at the dock in the morning. But I had a hard time falling asleep because I couldn't stop thinking about how great it would be if she did.

The next morning I showered and gathered up my things. I was waiting on the dock a few minutes before nine, and for the first time in almost a year I didn't feel excited about boarding the seaplane. I felt another crushing wave of loneliness, and suddenly my time on the island seemed kind of pointless.

I saw her when I turned around to grab my duffel bag. I stood up straight and watched her walk toward me, pulling a medium-size suitcase on wheels with one hand and gripping the handle of a black guitar case with the other. She was wearing a pair of shorts and a hot-pink T-shirt, and her hair was down.

No way.

When she reached me I smiled and said, "Well, I was wrong. You're much more adventurous than I thought."

She smiled back at me. "I told you not to make assumptions."

"Maybe I should have listened to you." I couldn't believe how happy I felt. For as much as I liked being alone, there was still a part of me that longed for companionship, especially from someone like her. She knew nothing about me but was still interested anyway. That hadn't happened in a long time.

I stopped smiling, though, when I noticed the blond guy who'd been sitting next to her at the bar last night walking toward us shouldering a large backpack and carrying a duffle bag.

What the hell?

She noticed me looking over her shoulder and turned around. "Oh, that's James," she said. "He was worried that you might be a serial killer and said he had no intention of letting me go to some uncharted island alone. You don't mind if he joins us, do you?"

Well, yeah. Kinda. But I understood. If I had been one of her traveling companions, I wouldn't have let her go off with some stranger, either. "No, it's fine," I said. I tried not to let my disappointment show. "I don't mind."

She beamed at me and I was glad she didn't pick up on how I really felt.

"I'm not a serial killer, though."

"Good to know," she said cheerfully. "I'll be sure to mention it to James."

The blond guy reached us. He set down his bag and thrust his hand out. "James Reed. Pleased to meet you. I hear we're going to be roughing it a bit. No worries. I'm quite adaptable. And you're lucky. My sister's the rare girl who doesn't worry much about luxuries."

His sister?

And just like that my good mood returned. I remembered their interaction at the bar. How he laughed and smiled when she teased him. I'd mistaken it for flirting but now I understood that they were just two siblings who actually liked one another. Of course he wouldn't let her come alone.

"It's nice to meet you, too," I said, shaking his hand a little too enthusiastically. James looked like he was a few years younger than Calia, but he was almost as tall as me, and solidly built. "I'm really glad you both decided to come," I said, now that I knew they were related. "It will be nice to have some company."

"Are we leaving soon?" James asked.

"Yes," I said. I pointed my finger. "Do you see that man over there? The one walking toward us eating a donut? That's Captain Forrester. He's our pilot. You'll like him."

"Good thing I ignored your rambling voice mail," he said when he reached us. "Thought you told me there'd only be one."

"Change of plans," I said. "This is Calia and her brother, James."

"Her brother, huh?" He looked at me pointedly and I turned away, hoping that Calia hadn't noticed. "Nice to meet you," he said, pumping both of their hands.

He was still chuckling quietly under his breath when I followed him to the cabin door.

"Oh, for God's sake. Stop it," I said.

"I can't help it," he said. "I've never known anyone who needed some company as badly as you do, son. I'm thrilled for you. Really." He flung open the door, turned back around, and sighed, shaking his head. "Too bad she's so damn ugly."

This time, I was the one who laughed.

I didn't sit up front. James and Calia sat next to each other and I sat across the aisle. It was hard to hear over the noise of the engines, so I mostly watched as they occasionally looked out the window, pointing out things to each other. It made me think of my sister, and how we used to get along like that when we were younger.

When we landed, James helped carry everything to shore. I was glad I'd made the call about the extra supplies. I still had quite a bit of nonperishable food, but we'd definitely need the water and other basic items that always needed restocking, like cooking fuel and paper products.

"You should have enough to get by for thirty days. When I make the next supply drop I'll bring a little extra of everything."

"Okay," I said. I shook his hand. "See you in thirty days."

The first thing I did when it was just the three of us was show Calia and James the house. James seemed fascinated, running his hands along the walls and opening and closing the door that connected the two rooms. "You built this all by yourself?" he asked. "How long did it take?"

"About nine months, give or take."

"Do you sleep here?"

"Sometimes. I mostly built the house so I'd have shelter from the storms during the rainy season. But you two can have the tent - it's much cooler and nicer to sleep near the beach. I don't mind sleeping in the house."

"Wicked job, mate."

"Thanks."

56

We made our way back to the beach. James seemed all in, but Calia was quiet and I worried that maybe she regretted her decision to come to the island. "I know it's a bit primitive," I said. "But there's a lot to do. We can snorkel and swim. I've got books and magazines. The dolphins will be here soon. You'll like them."

"I think it's fantastic," Calia said, surprising me.

"You do?"

"Yes. It isn't the five-star resorts that make places like this beautiful. It's when they're untouched that I like them the best. James and I much prefer places that are off the beaten path."

"Have you done a lot of traveling?" I asked.

"Loads," she said. "I picked a new place to explore every summer when I was at university. Something out of the ordinary. James loves it, too. It was his idea to come to the Maldives. Now we'll really get to experience it."

"Calia and I have a bit of wanderlust running through our veins," James said.

"We've always been a bit impulsive," Calia added.

"Mum didn't quite know what to do with us," James said.

"Mum didn't quite know what to do with *you*." Calia turned to me as if to explain. "Dad took off when we were young. Said he was going to the pub and never came back. Bastard. James quite fancied himself as the man of the house after that."

"I *was* the man of the house."

"In *theory*," Calia said gently. "You were only eleven." She looked at me. "That's probably why we're so open to trying new things. Mum worked two jobs to support us and wasn't home all that much. We ran a bit wild."

"What does she think about you coming here?" I asked. I assumed they'd called home, to let someone know of their change in plans. "Her only children on some remote island."

They shared a glance.

"She died four years ago," Calia said. "Now it's just James and me."

"And an uncle, Mum's brother," James added. "He was my legal guardian until a few months ago, when I turned eighteen.

But he's not all that interested in us anymore. Never has been, really."

"I'm sorry," I said. It struck me as significant that Calia was moving to Kenya to care for orphans when technically she was one herself. Maybe her dad was still very much alive, but Calia and James sure hadn't benefitted from his parenting in a very long time.

"It's fine," Calia said. "We're both adults. One of us only barely," she teased, poking James in the leg. "We were lucky. There was enough life insurance to pay for our education and for us to travel a bit. We'll settle down someday."

"My sister is going to save the world first," James said, his tone half mocking, half adoration.

I looked at him smiling at her and said, "There's nothing wrong with that."

We spent most of that first day in the water. I had stored Calia's suitcase and guitar in the house, and I walked her back to it so she could change. I waited outside and tried not to stare when she opened the door and stepped out wearing a tiny black string bikini. She was fairly tall, maybe five seven or eight, and her legs went on for miles.

She followed me through the woods back to the beach. I scanned the water, looking for the fins. The dolphins would be arriving soon, and I wanted to see the look on Calia's face when she met them for the first time. They still amazed me, even after a year's time.

James pointed at the snorkel mask and fins that I'd left lying on the sand. "Mind if I borrow them?" he asked.

"Not at all. You'll be amazed by what you see." I pointed out toward the reef. "Saw a whale shark out there one day. I swam with it until I was too tired to continue. It was absolutely incredible."

"That's wild," he said, bending down to pick them up. "Thanks."

"Be careful," I said. "The reef sharks won't bother you, but there's no telling what else you might encounter. Just pay attention, okay?"

"All right, mate. I will."

Calia and I watched him enter the water. Soon he was swimming toward the reef. I shielded my eyes from the sun with my hand. "It shouldn't be too much longer," I said.

"Until what?" she asked.

"You'll see."

We didn't have to wait long before I saw the first fin. Calia saw it, too, because I heard her sharp intake of breath.

"What is that, Owen?" Panicked, she looked toward the reef where James was snorkeling, ready to yell at him to get out of the water.

"It's okay," I said. "It's a dolphin. Keep your eye on that fin. There will be three or four more any minute."

"Look!" she said when the rest of them surfaced in the lagoon.

"Come on," I said. I started walking toward the shore.

She followed me. "Will they leave if we get in the water?"

"No. You're going to love this."

She was fascinated, just like I knew she would be, and even James took off the fins and mask long enough to meet them. I showed them how to gently stroke their stomachs when they turned over onto their backs, and catch a ride by holding onto their fins. Calia laughed when they splashed her. "Do they come every day?" she asked.

"Usually twice. Once in the late morning and once again in the afternoon. I feel bad when I'm not here, because they never miss a visit," I said. "They're the friendliest animals I've ever encountered."

When the dolphins left—as abruptly as they'd arrived—Calia and I swam in the lagoon for a while. I glanced at the sky and knew it was lunchtime by the position of the sun. "Are you getting hungry?" I asked.

"A little," she said.

"Do you like fish?"

"Sure."

She stood next to me in the water after I retrieved my fishing pole from the house and threw out my line. While we were waiting for a fish to bite I said, "The name Calia. It's unusual."

She rolled her eyes. "My mum named me."

"I've never heard it before."

"It's derived from the medieval Greek name Kaleas, which means 'good or beautiful person.'"

I stopped watching my fishing line long enough to look over at her. "Your mom chose well, because it's a perfect name for you."

This time there was no mistaking the flush on her cheeks. She looked over at me, smiled, and said, "Thanks, Owen."

James had enjoyed meeting the dolphins, but as soon as they left he was right back out at the reef. I had to yell at him to come in after I'd caught enough fish for our lunch.

"What's your story, Owen?" James asked while we were eating. "Calia said you're from California and that you've been here a whole year already."

"No story. Just felt like getting away," I said. "I go back to the mainland often enough that I'm never really bored."

"But don't you have a job? How do you afford the supplies then, mate? And the seaplane?"

"James," Calia scolded. "Don't be nosey."

"It's okay," I said. I turned toward James. "I planned ahead. Set some money aside. I can leave anytime."

"So you just left everything behind and came here?"

"Pretty much."

I'd been thinking a lot about what I might want to do next. I'd considered and then discarded half a dozen ideas. Nothing seemed interesting enough to convince me to start making plans. But going home to California hadn't even made the short list.

"I'm going for a swim," Calia announced. "Come with me, you lazy boys."

I was feeling a big sluggish after our meal, and apparently so was James. I wasn't surprised; I'd never seen someone eat so much in one sitting. Something told me he wasn't quite done growing yet.

"I'll join you in a few minutes, as soon as my stomach settles," he said.

"Same here," I echoed. She walked away, and I couldn't help but appreciate the view of Calia's backside in that tiny bikini.

James stretched out on the sand. "I know you thought you were only inviting Calia, so thanks for not minding that I came along," he said.

"No problem."

"I couldn't have let her come here alone."

Though he was only eighteen, I got the impression that James took his role as Calia's protector very seriously. "Of course not," I said.

"And she really wanted to come."

"She did?" I asked. I tried to make my voice sound bored, as if I really didn't care if she came or not. But something inside me perked up when he said that.

"Yeah. She said it sounded like the experience of a lifetime. The only time I've ever heard her more excited is when she talks about Africa. She *loves* Africa."

I looked toward the water. Calia was doing handstands and somersaults, and diving under the surface. I'd noticed that she rarely sat still. She'd fidgeted throughout lunch and always seemed to be moving. She must have noticed me watching her because she cupped her hands around her mouth and yelled, "Hurry up!"

James slowly raised his head when he heard her voice. Noticing his sister waiting impatiently for us to join her, he said, "Might as well get up. She's relentless."

"Is she always this energetic?" I asked.

He laughed and said, "Always."

Journal entry

June 5, 2000

James and Calia have been here for one week. I'm still not entirely sure why Calia wanted to come. She had to convince her brother to come with her, because there was no way he would have let her come alone. It would be great if part of the reason she wanted to come here was me.

She loves the dolphins. James loves to snorkel. I'm happier than I've been in a long time.

Journal entry

June 7, 2000

I let Calia and James have the tent, and I'm sleeping in the house. The tent was too small for the three of us. I told them they were welcome to join me, but the tent is more comfortable and the house isn't quite as inviting, especially at night. Maybe I can convince Calia to have a sleepover some night. I'm probably delusional.

Journal entry

June 8, 2000

Calia and I went swimming today. Not just messing around in the water, like we do all the time, but lap swimming. She held her own as we raced across the lagoon. When we finally stopped, both of us were breathing hard. I noticed her chest rising and falling with each breath, and I couldn't help but stare. She caught me looking, I know she did, but she didn't act like it bothered her.

I've never gone this long without sex, and I have never been this horny in my entire life, not even when I first figured out what sex was all about. But out of respect for James, I'm not going to make a move on his sister right in front of him. I can't imagine that being anything other than awkward.

But I will sure as hell capitalize on it if she makes one first.

Chapter 8A

T.J.

THE LOOK ON OWEN'S FACE right now, as he tells us about Calia and how he felt about her, what he hoped would happen between them, reminds me of the way I felt about Anna. How as time went by I hoped that something might happen between us, as ridiculous as that sounded because how could she ever see me as anything but a boy? How could she ever love me?

I remember watching her as I got older, searching for a change in the way she looked at me or the words she said. Anything that would let me know that she might feel the same way about me as I did about her. We lived under the constant threat of something going wrong, but nothing could erase the happiness I felt the day I discovered that Anna wanted me. When she told me it wasn't a one-time thing. How each day after that became easier because she was mine.

It all seemed so unfair, though. I loved her and she loved me, but our time together, as perfect as it was, would be cut short because we were both slowly starting to die. I remember Anna in her yellow bikini, so thin I could see every one of her ribs. I remember the smell of her hair the day I burned off eight inches of it. The look in her eyes on Christmas Day, when I realized she'd started to give up. The panic and fear that swept through me was worse than the fear I felt when the plane went down because there was no way to save ourselves this time.

There is nothing worse than realizing you're about to watch the girl that you've fallen in love with die.

And suddenly I have a very bad feeling about what Owen is going to tell us.

Chapter 9

Owen

"OWEN." CALIA SHOOK my shoulder, jarring me from sleep. "Wake up."

I kept my eyes shut. If I opened them it would be like admitting defeat.

"Let's go swimming," she said.

I liked to get up early, and Calia did, too. But I discovered that her idea and my idea of early were still about an hour apart. She'd started coming to the house at the crack of dawn to wake me up. James, however, rarely surfaced before noon. While I liked the alone time with her, I was experiencing a significant sleep deficit. Thank God I was covered by my sleeping bag from the waist down, otherwise she would have been able to see the condition I woke up in every morning, which was currently rock hard.

She started tickling me. Normally I would have hated that, but since she was touching me and I could imagine her hands doing other things I didn't really mind all that much. I opened my eyes and grabbed her hand, holding it firmly. "If I get up will you stop tickling me?"

She gave me a huge smile and nodded. "Now you're coming around."

"Is there coffee?" I'd shown her how to use the camp

stove. Maybe she'd already started the water boiling.

"Maybe," she said, drawing the word out. She tickled my ribs one more time and then bounded out of the house. I sat up, rubbed my eyes, and followed her.

James was still spending most of his time in the water, which left Calia and me alone for long periods of time. He really wanted to spot a whale shark. "I'm not going to stop until I see one," he'd said.

"I hope you do. I can't even describe how awesome it was to swim alongside something so huge."

Calia and I often watched him, his snorkel bobbing on the surface. "He won't stop until he sees one," she said. "He's very determined that way."

We were sitting in the shade one day a few weeks after Calia and James came to the island. I was reading an old issue of *Newsweek* while she strummed her guitar. We'd swum laps after lunch, and neither of us had wanted to be the first to quit. I was drowsy and contemplating taking a nap. Even Calia seemed a little tired.

"What's that song?" I asked. She strummed those same chords all the time, but I couldn't quite place it.

"'Un-Break My Heart' by Toni Braxton," she said.

"Yeah, that's it. Sing it for me."

"No."

"Why not?"

"I'm shy."

I snorted. "Bullshit. You are the opposite of shy. Just sing."

"Don't look at me," she said.

"Fine." I put down the magazine and stretched out on my back, closing my eyes. She strummed the guitar and just when I thought she'd changed her mind, she started to sing. I don't know what her hang-up was all about, because she sang the hell out of that song. I wasn't an expert by any means, but her voice sounded perfect and she hit every note.

I'd never listened to the words that closely before, and as she sang them I wondered why she'd chosen a song about heartbreak and pain. When she finished I opened my eyes and sat up. "Did some guy do that to you?" I asked. "Is that why you're always strumming that song?"

"No," she said softly. "I just think it's beautiful."

Reaching over, I took the guitar and placed it gently on the ground. She didn't say anything, but she looked into my eyes as if she was curious about what I might do next. I wanted to ask her why she'd come here. I wanted to ask her if there was someone waiting for her at home. I wanted to tell her that I thought *she* was beautiful.

And if James hadn't chosen that moment to run up to us, laughing and shaking droplets of water from his skin like a dog, I would have.

"Storm's coming tonight," James said. He was sitting in front of the camp stove heating up a can of beef stew when I walked up to him.

"Oh yeah?" I asked. "How do you know?"

"Your phone rang while I was in the house changing my clothes. Your pilot was on the other end. Said the barometer was dropping. Could be a big one."

There had been a few storms since I'd finished the house, but none that had ever prompted a call before. I glanced at the sky. Not a cloud in it. That didn't mean anything, though. I looked at James. "We better get everything moved inside the house."

"All right, mate. Let's batten it down."

After James finished eating, he, Calia, and I made several trips from the beach to the house. The sky gradually became overcast as we transported the camp stove, water, and supplies. I took down the tent and unhooked the solar shower from the tree.

Calia lagged behind when we carried our last load. I turned to see what was keeping her and noticed she was limping, probably because her feet were bare. "Where are your shoes?" I asked.

"I kicked them off back at the beach. I can't stand it when the sand gets between my feet and my flip-flops. I forgot to put them back on."

"You can't walk in the woods without shoes, Calia." The ground was covered with sharp sticks, thorns, and leaves; it was far different from the soft sand on the beach. "Let me see your feet." She placed a hand on my shoulder for balance, then showed me the soles of each foot. "They're a little red, but I don't think you've cut yourself," I said.

"It's not that far of a walk," she said.

"I know, but a cut could get infected easily here." I turned around. "Come on. I'll give you a piggyback ride the rest of the way and then I'll walk back to beach and get your shoes." She jumped up, grabbed on to my shoulders, and wrapped her legs around my waist. I hoisted her a little higher and began walking.

"I'm not too heavy, am I?" she asked.

I had no idea why girls always asked that, especially someone as slight as her. "You're incredibly heavy. I can hardly carry you."

She let go of me with one of her arms so she could hit me on the back of the head. "Don't be cheeky. Say, 'Calia is light as a feather.'"

I laughed. "Calia is light as a feather."

"She is the lightest, most delicate thing on the island."

"Wow, you're really laying it on thick," I said, which earned me another smack to the back of the head. "Ow! Will you stop that? One more hit like that and I may drop the delicate girl on her ass."

"I'm sorry. Please go ahead."

"Fine. You are the lightest, most delicate, most beautiful thing on the island." We'd reached the house by then. The front door hung open, but James was nowhere in sight. I walked across the threshold and set Calia down gently.

"I didn't say *beautiful*," she said.

"I know you didn't," I said.

She looked up at me, her smile wide. "You think I'm beautiful?"

I looked her in the eye. "Yes."

"I think you are, too." She turned red and got all flustered.

"I mean, I think you're very attractive. I like the way you look."

"Well thank God we got this out of the way," I said. She started laughing and we smiled at each other like we were relieved to no longer be carrying around this giant secret. "And just so you know, you'll get plenty of compliments from me without having to fish for them."

After I retrieved Calia's shoes we all made one last trip to the beach. Whitecaps were forming in the lagoon by then and the sky had faded into an eerie shade of pink. On the horizon, the skyline was turning a darker, more ominous color. When the rain began to fall we made our way quickly back to the house and ate peanut butter and crackers for dinner. I pulled out the bottle of whiskey that I'd added to one of my supply lists a few months ago, and we passed it around.

"That burns," Calia said, coughing and making a face.

"Sip it slowly. Don't take such a big drink," I said, taking my own turn when she handed me the bottle.

The whiskey relaxed me, but I didn't think it would be a good idea for any of us to drink too much of it, especially if Mother Nature really let loose. So far, there had only been some mildly worrisome sounds—and howling winds and torrential rain—but I'd made it through that kind of thing before, with just my tent for shelter. My biggest worry was that a tree would fall directly on us. I had no idea if the roof would hold.

"I know that Calia's going to Africa. But what are your plans, James?" I asked.

"Heading to uni in the fall." He took a drink of whiskey and handed the bottle to his sister. She waved him off so he passed it to me. "I want to be a successful businessman someday." He said it with total sincerity and all the enthusiasm you'd expect from an eighteen-year-old who had his whole life ahead of him.

"You like business, then?"

He laughed. "I like money." He had to raise his voice in order to be heard over the increasingly loud thunder. It sounded as if it was cracking directly over our heads.

Calia looked up at the roof, an uneasy expression on her face. She wrapped my blanket around her shoulders and scooted a little closer.

"It's okay," I said.

"We always had enough," James said. "But I want to own a big house and buy any car that catches my eye."

"Nothing wrong with that," I said. I wasn't going to caution him about everything that comes with wealth. Better to let him earn the money first.

"Did you go to uni, Owen?"

"I went to college in California. UCLA. I also studied business."

James perked up. "That's great, mate." His forehead wrinkled. "But if you don't mind my asking, why are you here? I mean, this place is ace and all, but why wouldn't you want to use your qualifications?"

"I did, for a while. Just felt like taking a break."

"You going back into business? After you leave here?"

I shrugged. "Not sure at this point." I'd already decided to leave when James and Calia headed back, sometime at the end of August. I wasn't sure what I wanted to do, but one thing I did know was that I was tired of being alone. The solitude I once couldn't get enough of had been replaced by a growing desire to put down roots somewhere, be around other people. I still had some time to decide where that would be.

Our conversation was interrupted when something hit the side of the house. The sound was so loud it was like something had exploded nearby and sent debris hurtling toward us like a series of missiles, one after the other. Adrenaline flooded my system and my heart rate increased. Calia screamed. The house shook and shuddered and creaked, and I almost expected all four walls to fall away, leaving us totally exposed to the elements.

Thankfully, that didn't happen. By then the three of us were huddled together, the blanket covering our heads. "My pilot told me he'd come if he ever thought there was a storm I couldn't ride out. I'm sure the worst of it will be over soon."

There were a few more loud crashes that made me hold

my breath for a second, but gradually the sounds lessened until finally, an hour later, we could hear only the rain.

James picked up the whiskey bottle. "That was wild," he said. He took a drink and handed it to me.

After I swallowed a sizeable amount I turned to hand it to Calia. She was still huddled under the blanket and when she looked up at me there were tears in her eyes. I felt a sudden stab of guilt because she hadn't signed up for this. "Hey," I said, placing a hand on her shoulder. "Don't worry. It's over."

James spoke up. "It's okay, sis. Just think of the story you'll be able to tell all your friends."

"I don't think this is the kind of story that will interest them," she said. But she valiantly attempted a smile and wiped her eyes with the back of her hand.

I wanted to pull her into my arms, hold her close, rub her back. But I didn't because of James. He had to know I was interested in his sister, otherwise why would I have invited her to come here? But I didn't think it would be a good idea to show his sister any affection when he was sitting right next to us. Plus it would feel really weird.

It was late by the time we made our bed on the floor, the three of us sleeping side by side, with Calia in the middle. James fell asleep quickly, his light snoring filling the room. Calia took longer, but finally her breathing deepened a little. As she lay beside me I wondered if she'd been thinking about the same things I was: How we'd pretty much admitted our attraction to each other. That left a logical next step, but James being here threw me off my game a little bit. I could try to find time to be alone with Calia, which would exclude James and make it seem as if we were hiding something. Or I could tell him point-blank that I was interested in his sister. I fell asleep considering my options.

I woke up when Calia started tossing and turning, bouncing between James and me like the silver ball in a pinball machine. But instead of just lying there doing nothing about it, I wrapped my arms around her and pulled her close, throwing one leg over her for good measure. She stopped moving and then sighed, as if all she really needed was someone to hold her.

She was still in my arms when I woke up the next morning, but at some point we'd both shifted, and she was now lying half on top of me, with her head on my chest and her leg wedged between mine, which felt incredible yet agonizing since there wasn't much I could do about it at the moment. I kept my eyes closed and focused on how good it felt with the weight of her on my body. I was highly aware of the rise and fall of our chests, our movements synchronized.

I turned my head when I heard a sound to my left. Surprisingly, James had woken up earlier than me and his sister for once. He looked at Calia lying in my arms, but his blank expression made it hard to determine what he was thinking. He left the house, shutting the door quietly behind him.

I started to ease Calia off of my chest, which woke her up. I had one hand up the back of her T-shirt and the other was wrapped around her upper arm. I wanted to pull the length of her as close to me as I could, and stroke her skin, but I held her gaze and said, "I need to go talk to your brother."

She raised her head a few inches and looked down at me. Her eyes were still half closed and her hair looked like someone had been running their hands through it all night. It made me wish the hands had been mine. "Okay," she said.

He was down by the water.

"Hey," I said.

"Hey." He must have grabbed the snorkel gear on his way out of the house because the mask hung around his neck. "So. You like my sister," James said.

I admired his direct approach. No beating around the bush for James. If he kept it up, he'd do just fine in business. "Well, I like you both," I said.

He bent down to slide his feet into the fins. "I mean you *like* her."

I looked him in the eye and nodded. "That, too. You okay with it?"

"Would it matter if I wasn't?" he asked.

He didn't use a hostile or accusatory tone. He sounded more like a guy who took the responsibility of making sure his sister was okay very seriously, and I remembered what Calia had said about James being the man of the house. From what I'd already observed, he'd done an outstanding job. He deserved my respect. "It would to me. Look, if my sister and I were as close as you and Calia, and it was just the two of us, I'd be paying very close attention to any guy that came near her. Just like you are. If I wasn't cool with something, I'd let him know. So don't hold back."

"Does she like you, too?" he asked.

"I think she might."

"Then that's good enough for me." He looked out toward the reef, shielding his eyes from the sun. "I like you, Owen. Calia's a great sister, but you make me wish I had a brother, too."

That choked me up a little. He'd been without a father since he was eleven, and he'd probably felt the weight of that no matter how hard his mother might have tried to convince him otherwise. I knew that feeling well, because my mom had tried her best to convince me of the same thing. James had risen to the challenge, though, which made me think he'd do just fine not only in business, but also in life.

"Thanks, James. That's really great of you."

He nodded. "Well, I'm gonna go see if that storm churned up a whale shark. One of these days I'll get lucky," he said.

"Maybe it'll be today." I patted him on the shoulder. "Be careful." I watched him walk into the water and then I turned back around and headed toward the house.

Chapter 10

Owen

CALIA WAS SHAKING OUT THE blanket and folding the sleeping bags when I returned. She piled them in the corner and said, "Did you talk to James?" Her tone sounded mildly curious, but the fact that she wouldn't stop moving made me think she'd built up some nervous energy.

"Yeah. It went just fine," I said.

She stopped moving. "Really?"

"Did you think it wouldn't? James hardly comes across as naïve. I don't think he was that surprised."

"No. It's just that I think he wishes he'd been born first so that he would be the oldest. He had to defer to me so many times when we were younger. He's eager to level the playing field, I think. He might have protested for reasons that had nothing to do with you and me."

"James will do just fine."

We gathered up a few things to take back to the beach. When we reached the sand I spotted James out near the reef. I'd never met anyone who loved being in the water as much as he did. "What if he'd minded?" Calia asked.

"What?"

"What if James *had* gotten upset?"

"Then I was prepared to tell him my arms were only around you because you're the most restless sleeper I've ever met, and if I didn't subdue you somehow, I'd never get any rest. Then I'd work on him until he came around."

"Was that the only reason I woke up in your arms?" she asked.

"Calia, I've wanted to wake up with you in my arms since the day you arrived."

She started laughing. "I'm so glad we got that out of the way, Owen."

The phone rang while we were collecting the last of the supplies from the house. When I answered it, Forrester said, "You all doing okay? That one ended up being a little worse than predicted. I was worried."

"It was intense," I said. "But we made it through okay. The house sustained some minor damage, but nothing I can't fix."

"Well, that's good to know. I'm still planning on making a supply drop two days from now. Do you have enough to last until then? Want me to bring anything in particular?"

Luckily, James and Calia had already walked back to the beach. "Yeah," I said. "I need you to bring condoms." Wishful thinking, maybe, but better safe than sorry.

"What's that?" he said.

"You heard me."

"Oh, I did, son. But I would love to hear you say it again," he said.

"I'm sure you would."

"So, do you have a brand preference?" I could hear him laughing. "Any special features you need me to look for?"

"I'm glad you think this is so amusing. I don't care what kind you bring. I'm hanging up now," I said. I hit the END button on the phone, but even I had to admit it was funny, in a mortifying kind of way.

We spent the day in the water. When the dolphins came, Calia held on to my shoulders while I held on to the fins of two dolphins swimming side by side. They towed us around the lagoon, which would have been entertaining by itself, but was even better when a pretty girl was hanging on tight.

The three of us went for a walk later, observing the damage left behind by the storm. Leaves littered the beach and several small trees had been blown over in the woods. Coconuts and breadfruit covered the ground. There were a few areas of the house that would need to be looked at, but the trees had done a good job of providing a barrier against some of the wind gusts.

That night, when the sun went down, we built a fire on the beach.

"Where's that whiskey, Owen?" James asked.

I went in search of the bottle and when I found it in the tent I walked back and handed it to him. After he took a drink he handed it back and I took a drink and then handed it to Calia. She didn't cough this time.

"Like a pro," James teased.

She was sitting close to me, and as we continued to pass the whiskey I felt more and more relaxed. My desire to be alone with Calia had simmered under the surface all day, and I was prepared to wait James out if I had to. It was a beautiful night and I had no intention of going to bed before he did. Staying up all night seemed like a small price to pay to be alone with her.

I had Calia to thank for what happened next. Maybe it was the whiskey or maybe she felt like hurrying things along because she crawled into my lap and wrapped her arms around my neck.

"And... I'm out," James said, standing up quickly. "Okay if I go sleep in the house? You guys can have the tent."

"Yeah, sure," I said somewhat distractedly, because Calia was in my lap.

"Good night, James," Calia called out cheerfully.

"Nice," I said. I cupped her face in my hands and kissed her, and the minute our lips met I had to force myself not to lose all control. It had been so long since I'd been with anyone. She ran her hands through my hair and kissed me back. I smelled the ocean on her skin and tasted the faint trace of whiskey on her tongue. I stopped kissing her just long enough to move her legs so that she straddled me. I hadn't thought this could feel any better than it already did, but I was wrong.

Calia was breathing as hard as I was by then, and her breathing grew even more ragged when I swept her mouth with my tongue. I put my hands in her hair and wound some of it around my fingers, then pulled gently so that her head tipped back and her neck was exposed. Sucking gently on the skin right below her jaw, I listened to her moan, which only made me want to do other things to her, things that would make her moan even louder.

After a few minutes she broke away to return the favor. She traced a path with her tongue from my ear to my jawline and finally down to my neck. When she started to suck I nearly lost my mind.

We continued to kiss for what seemed like hours, but even then I could not get enough. She was wearing a tank top and jeans, with a zip-up hoodie to keep the bugs from biting her arms. Entirely too much clothing in my opinion. I unzipped her hoodie and pushed it off her shoulders, watching as she finished removing it. I pulled her tank top over her head, and I was unbelievably happy when I discovered she wasn't wearing a bra. The moon was like a spotlight shining down on her, making it easy for me to look at what I'd been dying to see, to touch. I ran my hand from her collarbone down to her stomach, and she groaned when my palm skimmed her nipple on the way. I cupped her breasts and used my thumbs, my tongue, and my mouth to make her shout, "Oh God, Owen," as she grabbed fistfuls of my hair.

I was just about to pop the button on her jeans when she stopped me by placing her hand on my wrist and gently pulling on it. "Tomorrow," she said, trying to catch her breath.

"Okay," I said, kissing her slowly one last time. It was probably better that we stopped, considering my condoms hadn't arrived yet.

She leaned forward, laying her head on my chest. I was sure she could feel my heart pounding under her cheek as I held her close, thinking that nothing had felt this good in a long time.

"Are you ready to go to bed?" I asked. Just being able to ask her that made me happy, because tonight she'd be sleeping in my arms again.

"Yes," she answered. I handed her tank top to her and waited while she put it back on. She climbed off my lap and I stood up and offered her my hand. She grabbed it and I pulled her up, lacing my fingers with hers as we walked to the tent. Once we were inside, I clicked on the flashlight and handed it to Calia. "Hold this please," I said. I took the two sleeping bags and zipped them together, making one large one for us to share. "You can shut it off now." I held the bag open so she could slide inside. "I won't take advantage of the situation if you want to take off your jeans," I said.

"A perfect gentleman," she said, wriggling out of them as soon as she was covered by the sleeping bag.

The thoughts running through my head were not those of a gentleman, not even close. I'd been without physical contact for way too long and right then I was as close to being in agony as I'd ever been. But I wasn't going to tell her that, make her feel like she owed me anything because she didn't. I was wearing a sweatshirt, and before I slipped in beside her I pulled it over my head. I left my shorts on because my self-control had a limit, and stripping down any further would test it severely. I pulled her into my arms and listened to her contented sigh as I stroked her hair.

Before I'd come to this island I told myself that if being alone was what I really wanted, I'd have to be willing to give up *all* relationships. And that was kind of a problem because I really liked having a girlfriend by my side. But I'd convinced myself that I could get by without one, at least for a little while. I was wrong though, because holding Calia in my arms, and kissing her, made me realize that I wasn't willing to give this up again, not in the foreseeable future, and not voluntarily. This carefree girl had already gotten under my skin, caused me to look at things differently. Maybe it wasn't about being alone. Maybe the answer wasn't about hiding from those who wanted something, but about finding those who needed help but would never considering asking.

And doing it alongside a beautiful girl who just wanted to save the world.

Chapter 11

Owen

I WORRIED IT MIGHT BE awkward the next day, but James went about his business as usual, probably trying not to think about the fact that I'd spent the night with his sister. Calia and I kept to our same routine, too: We swam, we hung out with the dolphins, and we talked.

That night, I couldn't wait to be with Calia again. I'd stolen a few kisses when James was out snorkeling, but for the most part we'd kept our hands off of each other. The anticipation of what we'd do as soon as we were alone made it hard for me to concentrate, and as soon as James said good night and took off for the house, I pulled Calia into my arms. Maybe she felt the same way, because I didn't have a chance to say anything to her before her mouth was on mine. My need for her was every bit as strong, and I didn't think it was entirely because of how long I'd gone without someone to kiss and hold. Everything Calia did seemed like it came from a passionate place, as if she didn't do anything halfway. She hadn't let me get as far as I'd wanted the night before, but she hadn't held anything back right up to the point where she'd stopped me, either.

We'd been standing on the beach when James left, but as soon as the kiss ended I took her by the hand and pulled her into the tent.

We fell on each other like a couple of horny teenagers. Either it had been a while for her, too, or we were just lucky enough to be on the same exact page at that moment. Gone was the exploratory feel of the night before. I anticipated—or at least I hoped—that she'd let me do the same things I'd already done, and that knowledge alone prompted me to get her out of her shirt immediately. I groaned when she stripped off mine equally fast.

I kissed my way from her lips to her neck and then her shoulder. I slowly ran my hands along the surface of her exposed skin, listening to the sounds she made. She did the same, and I groaned when she stretched out on top of me and pressed the length of her body down on me. I was so hard it was painful, and I worried I might come in my shorts right then. As great as that would have felt, I actually wanted to wait for the real thing.

I rolled her off of me and this time, when I tugged on the button of her jeans, she didn't stop me. I unzipped them and pulled them off. She reached over and tried to do the same to me, but this time it was me that stopped her.

"I don't have any condoms," I said.

"I don't either," she said.

"I put them on the supply list. They'll be here tomorrow."

"You asked your pilot to bring condoms?"

"Yes," I said. "And I'd prefer not to have that conversation ever again. I'm trying to pretend the first one never happened."

She started laughing. "You're amazing," she said. "I don't mind waiting. Really, it's okay. It will just feel that much better."

"You don't have to wait. There are plenty of ways I can make you feel good that don't require a condom." I kissed her lips and then her neck. I worked my way down her body, making a leisurely stop at her chest and her stomach. I hooked my thumbs under the waistband of her underwear and pulled them down slowly, and my mouth traveled lower still as I showed her exactly what I meant.

And afterward, she insisted on removing the rest of my clothes and showing me just how thankful she was.

Chapter 12

Owen

THE THREE OF US WERE sitting on the beach when we heard the noise of the seaplane. Once it was idling in the lagoon we waded out to help carry the supplies to shore. Inside one of the boxes was a brown paper bag and I grabbed it and stuffed it in my duffel bag.

Once everything was unloaded we sat together under the shade of the tree and talked for a while. "I need to leave soon," Forrester said. "Got a plane full of girls to fly to one of the resorts."

"Fly 'em here," James said. "I'm horny as hell."

"James!" Calia said.

"Well, it's the truth. Besides, you're one to talk."

"You find that whale shark yet, James?" Forrester took a handkerchief out of his pocket and mopped his face. "That'll keep your mind off the girls."

"Not yet. But I will."

"I brought everything you asked for, Owen," he said pointedly. I half expected him to wink at me.

"Yes, I saw that. Thank you."

"Just let me know if you need more."

"I'll do that."

"Well, you kids have fun. I got things to do, people to fly."

James and I shook his hand. "Thanks," we said. Calia gave a little wave and then we watched him wade back to the plane and take off.

If waiting for night to fall the evening before had been hard, now the wait seemed endless. All I could think about was being alone with Calia, and how we wouldn't have to stop this time.

When we were in the water after swimming our laps I picked her up and she wrapped her legs around me. James wasn't around, so I kissed her, enjoying the noises she made when I pulled her even closer. "I'm halfway there, Owen," she said. "Just thinking about it."

I laughed and said, "And I am even closer than that."

Finally, when we'd had dinner, gone for one last swim, showered the ocean water from our skin, watched the nightly bat show, eaten the candy bars that always arrived with our fresh supplies, and had one last drink of water, it was time to go to bed.

Calia followed me into the tent and I took her in my arms without speaking. I kissed her, on her mouth, down her neck, on her ear, her collarbone. Anywhere her skin was exposed. I wanted to rip her clothes off and skip all the other steps, but I forced myself to slow down so that it would be just as good for her.

She rolled on top of me and straddled my body. I watched as she pulled her shirt over her head and then leaned down so I could continue kissing that bare skin. I eased her off of me so I could unzip her jeans and pull them down, taking her underwear with them, touching her, already starting to become familiar with the way she wanted me to use my hands and mouth. Soon, I scrambled out of my own clothes, forgetting what I'd told myself about going slow. "I want you," I said. "Right now."

She was breathing so hard she could hardly speak. "I want you, too," she managed to say while stroking me, which almost made me come right then and there. I grabbed a condom and tore it open with my teeth, and almost instantly I was inside her. She moved with me and she felt so incredible. It took everything I had to concentrate on not coming and just when I thought there was no way I'd be able to hold back any longer, she went a little crazy, making these little noises and moving faster and faster until she cried out. Less than a minute later, I came, too, groaning and saying her name as I pulsed inside her.

We were covered in sweat and breathing hard, and when our heart rates returned to normal we laid together with our arms and legs wrapped around each other. I ran my fingers through her hair, wrapping it idly around my fingers. "Is there someone at home?" I said. "Someone who's waiting for you?"

"No," she said. "No one special. What about you?"

"No."

"Did you have a girlfriend before you came here?"

"Yes."

"What was her name?"

"Chelsea."

"So you broke up?"

"I asked her to come with me. She declined." Chelsea liked the cocktail parties and being photographed with me. She liked nice dinners and expensive jewelry. She *loved* my BMW. The look of absolute horror on her face when I told her I was leaving the company was enough to make me realize that Chelsea liked my lifestyle a lot more than she liked me. When I tested my theory by asking her to come here with me she didn't even bother to hide her feelings. "That's insane, Owen," she'd said.

"I guess that's a no, then," I'd responded.

I reached for my water and took a drink, then handed it to Calia. "Thirsty?"

She took the bottle. "Thanks."

"How long will you stay here with me?" I asked.

"Until the end of August, maybe the first week of September. I've got some things to take care of before James starts university at the end of September. I'll leave for Africa at the beginning of October."

That was still a few weeks away. "Okay," I said. I kissed her again and fell asleep with her in my arms.

Almost everything I did from that day on, I did with Calia next to me. When we laid side by side on the sand, the sky above me looked bluer. When we swam with the dolphins, the water seemed clearer. At mealtimes, the food tasted better although there was no logical reason why it would. Every time she smiled at me—and she smiled at me a lot—made me feel hopeful. Instead of thinking I was some strange, eccentric recluse, she'd accepted my explanation and my need for solitude at face value and then come along for the ride, simultaneously satisfying her own need for adventure. And wasn't that how it was supposed to be? The mind-blowing sex was just an awesome, added bonus.

My feelings for her intensified with each day we spent together. She made me happy and it had been a really long time since anyone—or anything—had made me feel that way.

We were sitting on the beach talking. The seaplane would be returning to pick up Calia and James in seven days, and I wanted to run something by her. "When do you get back from Africa?" I asked.

"The end of May."

"What are you going to do after that?"

"I don't know," she said. She reached over and grabbed my hand. "I haven't decided yet. What are you going to do?"

"I don't want to stay here after you leave. It won't be the same. I thought I'd rent a place in Malé. Hang out for a while. Maybe visit Thailand."

"Owen?" She sounded worried. "Do you think you could wait for me?"

"Of course I'll wait for you," I said.

She sighed. "I was hoping you would say that."

I put my arm around her and kissed the top of her head. She leaned back against me and we sat like that until James started yelling. I couldn't understand what he was saying, so I shielded my eyes with my hand in order to get a better look.

He was bobbing up and down awkwardly, hitting the surface of the water with his hand. "Calia," I said.

"Hmmm?" She sounded drowsy, like she was about to doze off in my arms.

"What is James doing out there?" I eased her off of me and stood up quickly, watching as James finally started swimming toward shore. "James," I yelled. "Are you okay?" That got Calia's attention, and she rose to her feet.

"What's wrong?" she asked.

A wave of panic rolled over me, because he didn't answer me. "James!"

"Why isn't he answering you?" Calia asked, and I could hear the sudden alarm in her voice. She yelled his name repeatedly, her voice sounding more hysterical by the second.

He'd been swimming steadily toward us, but his pace had started to slow and his arms and legs were no longer moving in synchronization. I ran into the water, heart pounding, because I knew in my gut what had happened, and the pool of blood surrounding him confirmed my fear that he'd been bitten by something, most likely a shark.

I swam toward him as fast as I could, hoping that I wasn't swimming toward the same fate as James but knowing there was no way I could leave him in the water.

Calia's screams intensified, so I knew she could see the blood from the shore. When I reached James he stopped swimming and threw an arm over my shoulder. His eyes were glazed and unfocused. "I'm here, James," I said. "I'm going to get you to the shore and then everything will be okay." I talked myself into believing that, even though there was so much blood in the water it seemed as if the entire lagoon had turned red. The amount of adrenaline pumping through my body made it feel like the journey took only seconds, although in reality it was probably closer to a minute. I dragged him through the water as fast as I could, afraid to look behind me for fear of what I'd see.

When I was ten feet from shore Calia ran screaming into the water and we pulled James onto the sand. I knew right then that it was already too late for him. I knew it by the lack of color in his skin. By the way his pupils were fixed. Because of the wide gash on his upper thigh and the way we could see the blood pumping from it through the jagged tear in his shorts, soaking into the white sand.

Calia held her hand tight against the wound as if trying to literally keep her brother's life inside him, to keep it from escaping by sheer force. "It's okay, James. It's okay. Everything will be okay," Calia said. She kept saying it over and over, but James didn't answer her.

I thought about telling Calia to get the satellite phone. I thought about running to get it myself. I thought about finding something to use as a tourniquet, to stop the blood that was flowing out of him at an alarming rate. But in the end I didn't do either of those things, because even if a seaplane had been idling in the lagoon with a team of paramedics on board, it would have been too late.

James had lost consciousness by then. The bleeding slowed and finally stopped and then I watched in horror as the rise and fall of James's chest stopped, too. I pressed my fingers to his neck, hoping desperately for a pulse, but feeling nothing.

I would never forget the sound of Calia's crying.

She stretched out next to her brother and wrapped her arms around him. She stayed by James's side, despite the heat and the strength of the afternoon sun. I felt absolutely powerless to help her, but I stayed with her, not speaking, wondering just what the hell we were supposed to do next. Finally I said, "I'll be right back. I'm going to get the satellite phone." She didn't answer me and I was afraid she might be going into shock, so I hurried back to the tent and grabbed the phone from my bag. I hit the button and nothing happened. The lights didn't even come on, and I realized the battery was dead. I'd charged the phone the last time I'd stayed at the hotel, and there should have been enough battery power to last for another month or two, but something had obviously gone wrong.

This is not happening.

But it was. And it would be a week before the seaplane would be coming back for us. I held my head in my hands and tried to think. I needed to attend to Calia. And I needed to do something about the body that was lying in the hot sun. But before I could do anything at all I bolted out of the tent and

puked. That had always been my body's go-to method for dealing with stress. My mom used to say it was the only way she
ever knew that something was bothering me.

As soon as I stopped dry-heaving, I stood up. There was a
girl on the beach who needed me to comfort her, to figure out
what we were going to do. I walked back to Calia and sat down
beside her.

"I'm trying to get a hold of my pilot. He's not… answering
right now, but I'm sure he'll pick up later. I'll try again soon." I
didn't have the heart to tell Calia the phone battery was dead.
She didn't acknowledge me; she just kept staring at her brother
lying there on the sand. "I need to move James," I said, as gently as I could.

"No," she said. She looked at me and I saw the anxiety on
her face, the fear. Her voice sounded panicky and tears ran
down her face. "Not yet, Owen. Leave him here a little while
longer. Please."

I knew that there was probably a small part of her that was
processing what the heat and the direct sunlight would do to
James's body. But I also knew that there was an even larger part
that wasn't ready to let him go. How could I deny her?

"Whatever you want," I said.

So we remained on the beach. The smell of blood was all
around us, metallic and sharp. Filling my nose with the smell of
death. But still she stayed by his side, so I stayed by hers.

Finally, hours later, when the sun began to sink lower in
the sky, she took a big breath and let it out slowly. "Where will
you take him?" she asked.

"To the cave." I'd shown Calia and James the cave one day
when we'd walked by it. James had crawled inside with the
flashlight, the way I had when I first discovered its existence.
Calia had wanted no part of it. She'd poked her head in and
retreated immediately, shuddering.

"He'll be safe there," I said. The heat and humidity
wouldn't be kind to James's body, no matter where I moved
him, but it felt like the most respectful thing to do.

Calia placed a kiss on James's forehead, then stood up and
said, "Okay, Owen. You can take him now." I watched as she

walked to the tent and disappeared inside.

Steeling myself for the job, I took a deep breath, which was a big mistake because it only drew the smell deeper into my lungs. My stomach gave one halfhearted lurch, but there wasn't anything in it to puke up and eventually the urge subsided.

I grabbed James under the arms and started dragging him into the woods. It had been about six hours since he'd died, and rigor mortis had already set in; his body felt stiff and unyielding.

When I reached the cave I cleared the debris away from the opening. I looked down at him once last time and swallowed hard. I said, "I'm so sorry, James," and pushed his body all the way in; there was really no gentle way to do it. After piling sticks in front of the opening to form a makeshift barricade, I stood up and walked away.

When I returned to the beach I lit a fire and threw my bloody clothes into it, then stood under the solar shower until my skin was clean. After I dressed, I crawled into the tent to check on Calia.

Amazingly, she was asleep. Her cheeks were sunburned after sitting on the beach all day, and while I knew she probably wouldn't eat anything, I wanted her to drink some water. I'd forced myself to drink some while I stood beside the fire, and I was relieved when I kept it down.

But maybe it was better if she slept. Maybe that was her body's way of dealing with the stress. I lay down next to her, listening to her slow and steady breathing. At one point she cried out in her sleep, and my body tensed, preparing for another round of tears. I put my arms around her and drew her close. She didn't wake up, though. She clung to me and finally her grip loosened as she drifted into a deeper sleep. I held her all night long, dozing fitfully, trying to erase the memory of the terrible things that had happened on the beach.

When Calia woke up early the next morning, I helped her out of the tent. She shielded her eyes against the bright light of the sun and her knees buckled. I caught her before she fell. "Let's get some water," I said. She let me lead her over to where we kept the water. Once she sat down, she looked around, scanning the beach as if she was searching for someone. I crouched beside her, uncapped the water, and held it to her mouth. She drank reflexively at first, but then her thirst kicked in and she took the bottle from my hands, draining it. "Do you want some more?" I asked.

"No, thank you," she said. Her eyes seemed unfocused and her voice sounded raspy from the crying. I put my arm around her, which seemed to comfort her. "After I hear back from my pilot I'll have him come get us and take us to the hotel, okay? I left him a message. I'm sure he'll be calling very soon."

"Okay," she said. I hated lying to her, but maybe it didn't matter because her tone was apathetic at best. I could have told her anything and she probably would have responded the same way.

"Do you think you can eat something?" I asked.

"No."

"Do you want to rinse off?" She was covered in James's dried blood. Her arms and legs were streaked red, and her shorts and shirt were tacky with it; it seemed to be everywhere. There was no way she'd go in the water, but I could have put her under the shower and dressed her in clean clothes.

"I just want to sit, Owen."

So we sat in the shade under the tree all morning, not talking. At one point I realized Calia had fallen asleep again, slumped against me, so I laid her down with her head in my lap. I stared out at the water, and I no longer noticed the vibrant color or the clear shallows. I could only see the image of blood staining the water a cruel red.

The sky became overcast an hour later and at first I didn't think anything of it. During the rainy season, it wasn't uncommon for there to be periods of showers off and on throughout the day. Sometimes the rain fell while the sun still shone, and sometimes the clouds rolled in suddenly, rolling out just as fast when the rain ended.

But the sky darkened and the rain didn't come. The wind picked up a little and churned the water in the lagoon, and I could almost feel the drop in barometric pressure. I'd thought that things couldn't possibly get worse, but of course they could; they always could. I felt like screaming at the sky.

I roused Calia, but she didn't seem to register the approaching storm. I had to start preparing, which would be more difficult since I'd be moving everything by myself.

"The weather's turning a bit," I said, trying to downplay the situation. "It will probably blow through fast, so don't worry." I didn't want to alarm her, but Calia looked at me with fear in her eyes, and I remembered the tears I'd seen in them during the last storm. "It'll be okay," I said. But I honestly didn't know how much more she could take.

I stood up and had taken a few steps toward the tent when I heard the sound: the twin engines of a seaplane. The relief that swept through me was immeasurable, and it grew as the plane suddenly came into view, dropping out of the clouds and landing in the lagoon. When I looked back on it later, I wondered if there had been some kind of divine intervention. Like the universe had decided we'd suffered enough, so it sent us the one thing I had always dreaded but actually needed right then: a storm we couldn't ride out.

"Stay here," I said to Calia, though probably didn't need to, because she didn't seem as if she had the ability to follow me.

The door to the seaplane was already open when I reached it. He took one look at my face and said, "It's okay, son. I told you I'd come get you if the weather got too bad. I tried to call but you didn't answer.

"James is dead," I blurted. "He got bitten by something, a shark probably, and bled to death." I thought telling someone would make me feel better, but it didn't. It made it seem more real, more horrifying. Especially when I saw the expression on Captain Forrester's face. I'd never seen him look shocked before, but that's what I was seeing now. "I don't... I don't know what to do," I yelled. "I don't know what the fuck to do!"

"Okay, calm down. Listen," he said, glancing toward the

beach where Calia was lying slumped over on the sand. "The first thing we're going to do is pack up and head back before this storm really lets loose. We'll worry about what to do next when we get there." He jumped into the water and looked over his shoulder at me. "Come on, son."

It took several trips. We hurried back and forth to the seaplane carrying the camp stove, the tent, Calia's and my suitcase, James's backpack, and the tent. The beach showed no sign of anyone having been there except for the large red stain on the sand that the rain would wash away.

The first crack of thunder came when I was about to walk into the woods. "There are some things in the house," I said.

"Anything you can't replace?" he asked with some urgency. "We really need to get going."

I mentally inventoried the contents of the house: Calia's guitar, my toolbox, James's sleeping bag, and a few of his clothes.

"No."

"Then leave it behind."

I carried Calia to the seaplane and once I got her inside I buckled her in tight. She laid her hand on my arm, gripping it tight.

"We can't leave him," she said.

"We have to, Calia." I picked up her hand and held it between both of mine. "We don't have any choice."

The wind and rain battered the small plane and the lightning lit up the sky. If I hadn't already been dealing with one traumatic event, I might have worried about the thunder that sounded like a bomb going off every few seconds. Maybe I should have worried that the plane would crash, but I didn't.

If you'd asked me right then, I might have said I was pretty sure Calia wouldn't have cared if it did.

When we finally landed I helped secure the seaplane to the dock.

"I got you a room at the hotel," Captain Forrester said. "Go. Take care of her and call me when you get settled."

Inside the seaplane, I unbuckled Calia. "I need you to come with me," I said. I hated that my voice sounded so stern, but she had to walk under her own power because I'd have my hands full until I could get us checked in.

I slung my duffel bag over my arm and pulled our two suitcases behind me as the rain pelted us. The only positive is that it washed some of the blood from Calia's skin so we wouldn't look like something out of a horror film when we walked into the hotel.

I sat her on a bench in the lobby and once I had the room key I motioned her to follow.

When we entered our room I closed the door behind us, went into the bathroom, and filled the tub with warm water. Calia was sitting on the edge of the bed, not crying, not speaking. Just sitting there. I pulled her gently to her feet and she put her hand in mine and let me lead her to the bathroom. I took off her clothes and helped her step into the tub.

"Please don't leave," she whispered.

"I'm not going anywhere. I'll do whatever you need me to do," I said. Using my cupped hands, I scooped up water and let it run down her scalp until her hair was wet. I washed her hair and her body and when the water turned pink I quickly drained the tub. I turned the taps on again and filled it with fresh water, which stayed clear this time. "Are you warm enough?" I asked.

She nodded and laid her head against the back of the tub, so I stripped off my clothes and stepped into the stall shower on the opposite side of the room. After quickly washing myself, I wrapped a towel around my waist and knelt down beside her. Her eyes were closed.

"Let's get you dried off," I said, helping her out of the tub. "Okay."

I patted her skin with a towel and grabbed one of the robes from the closet, wrapping it around her and leading her back to the bed. After I pulled back the covers she slid between the sheets and curled into a ball. "I'm going to order some food and it would really make me feel better if you could try to eat something." Neither of us had eaten since breakfast the day before, and though I had no appetite, my stomach felt empty and hollow. "Do you want to try some soup?"

She nodded. "Can you order me some hot tea?"

"Of course."

She tried, she really did. She managed to swallow some of the soup and all the tea. After that she burrowed down into the covers and went back to sleep, and eventually I joined her.

When I opened my eyes the next morning Calia was already awake. When she felt me stir she turned toward me. Her eyes were red and swollen, but she didn't start crying again. "I miss him, Owen. I just miss him so much."

"I know you do." I pulled her closer. She rested her head on my chest and I rubbed her back. "Tell me what you want to do and I'll make it happen."

"I want to go home. I want to be where everything is familiar. Where James's things are. Pictures of him. Things of his that I can smell and touch. I need that."

"Then I'll take you there," I said.

"It's okay," she said. "I know it seems like I'm barely functioning, but I can do this. I can get there on my own. I feel a bit better now, really.

"What about your uncle? Do you want me to call him? He may want to make arrangements... send someone to retrieve the body."

She winced when I said that. "He won't care," she said. "He won't want to be bothered. Mum has a friend named Sally. They've been close since they were young girls, like sisters almost. She always told me I was like a second daughter to her. I'll call her. She'll know what to do."

"Do you still have your plane ticket?" I asked.

"It's in my suitcase."

"I'll take care of switching your flight."

"It's my fault," she said suddenly, like the knowledge had been pressing down on her and she couldn't hold it in one more second. "I told him I wanted to go to the island and when he said he wouldn't let me go alone I begged him to come with me. What have I done, Owen?"

I pulled her into my arms, and this time, her tears did fall again. "You didn't do anything, Calia. You didn't do anything at all."

Because if James's death was anyone's fault, it was mine.

Chapter 12A

Anna

I FEEL AS IF MY heart will break in two. The look on Owen's face is almost more than I can bear, and I can tell without a doubt that his remorse runs miles deep. T.J. holds me in his arms as I cry silent tears for Owen, and for Calia, and especially for James.

I think about how many times T.J. and I were in danger and probably didn't even know it. How many times were there sharks nearby that decided to leave us alone? Was the shark that bit James simply reminding him that he was in their territory? Maybe it was an exploratory bite but in the worst possible place, resulting in an injury far beyond Owen and Calia's life-saving abilities. James took risks the same way T.J. sometimes had while we were on the island. I'd been so angry the day I discovered him standing waist-deep in the water when he knew it was dangerous. I accused him of acting as if he were invincible. Maybe James thought he was invincible, too.

I'm torn between the relief that T.J. never had to pay for his actions with his life with the knowledge that James did. It all seems so random, arbitrary, unfair. A perfect storm of things that went wrong.

I simply can't imagine what it had been like for all of them on the beach that day. Owen's expression, full of heartache and pain and anguish, tells me that I probably never will.

Chapter 13

Owen

CALIA'S PLANE WAS SCHEDULED TO take off at 5:00 P.M.

"I can go with you," I said. "I'll help you when you get home, make some calls, do whatever you need me to do." I didn't want to be in her way, and I sensed that she needed to be alone with James's memory for a while, but it still felt wrong to just put her on a plane.

"I've got a few great girlfriends who will help me. I know I seem helpless, Owen, but I can do this." She smiled at me. It was a weak smile, and it required some effort on her part, but it was a hell of an improvement from the almost-catatonic state she'd been in.

"I'll go back and get him," I said. It took a minute for my words to sink in, but then she seemed to understand.

"You will?" she asked.

"Yes."

There was no disguising the hopeful expression on her face, and I realized that this was the one thing I *could* do for her. "When?"

"Whenever you want me to. I can go right away, or I can wait." My words sounded braver than I felt. Maybe a better man wouldn't have let anything stop him, but there was a part of me that could hardly stomach the thought of going back for James in the next couple of days, after the island heat and humidity had kicked his decomposition into high gear. But I would have, if she had said the word.

Calia must have been thinking about that, too, because she looked anxious and scared. "I don't want to see him like that."

"I understand."

"He'll be okay, won't he?"

"Yes. No one is going to touch him or move him, or even know that he's there. I can stay here, maybe bum around Thailand for a while, and then go back for him next June, after you return from Africa. Then we'll bury him." I didn't know how long it would take James to decompose fully, but that should be enough time to do it. I didn't know the legalities involved in transporting human remains, either, but I had plenty of time to find out.

"There's a small cemetery not far from my home. I would like to bring him there, Owen. I would like that a lot."

"Okay. That's what we'll do then."

Calia reached into her bag and pulled out a phone. "Program your number into my mobile."

I typed in my contact information and hit SAVE, then handed it back to her.

"Thank you for being willing to bring James home," she said.

"I'd do anything for you, Calia," I said, and then I hailed a cab and we went to the airport.

Right before her boarding call, I took her face in my hands and kissed her softly. Then I pulled her close and whispered in her ear. She whispered a response in mine, hugged me one last time, and walked onto the plane.

She never called.

I expected her to let me know that she'd arrived in Farnham safely, and my cell phone was never far from my side those first few days. I checked it repeatedly, in case I'd somehow missed her call.

At first I told myself that she was probably busy trying to deal with all the things that would need her attention, and she'd

98

just forgotten.

But how could you forget to make a call like that?

I also expected an outraged phone call from Calia's uncle. She said he wouldn't care, but how could you not care about something like that? How could you not attempt to bring your nephew's body home, regardless of the relationship you had with him?

What I didn't expect was to receive no call at all.

After she'd been gone a week I had my own version of a breakdown. I'd rented a small place in Malé after I checked out of the hotel, and it felt as if the walls were literally closing in. I was consumed by despair, and I'd convinced myself that Calia blamed me for James's death, regretted ever crossing my path. That she didn't have any intention of calling me but hadn't wanted to hurt my feelings.

I felt utterly selfish and completely adrift. I couldn't get past the fact that I'd ruined everything for Calia. My choices had inadvertently ended the life of the only person she had left in the world. The guilt and the remorse came crashing down and there were days when I could hardly get out of bed.

When it seemed like I had done nothing but sleep for weeks, I made myself get up. I didn't want to, but I did. I took a shower and got dressed and I went outside for five minutes. Then I went inside and went back to bed. But the next day I got up again and I went for a walk through the streets of Malé. I made myself get out of bed every day after that, and eventually, I didn't have to try that hard anymore. I did travel then, monthlong trips to Thailand and Sri Lanka, Vietnam and Cambodia. The traveling helped to pass the time.

When June rolled around I made a phone call, just like I'd promised Calia. "I need you to fly me back to the island."

"Why, son? Why do you want to go back there?"

"Because I said I would."

He didn't try to talk me out of it. He agreed to help me, the way he always had. "Meet me at the seaplane dock at 9:00 A.M. tomorrow, Owen."

Just like old times.

I waited for him all morning, but he never showed. When I saw a group of pilots huddled together on the dock talking, I asked them if they knew anything.

And that's when I found out that Captain Mick Forrester's seaplane had gone down in the ocean carrying two people from Chicago.

Chapter 14

Owen

ANNA AND T.J. don't say anything at first, and in the silence I swear I can hear the ticking of my watch. My throat burns from talking so long, and my voice is hoarse.

Anna leaves the room and returns with a glass of ice water. She hands it to me and I drink half of it before setting down the glass. I make myself keep talking, because I haven't told them the worst part.

"There's more," I say. "I knew where the island was located. I'd asked one day when we were flying back from one of the supply runs. I didn't understand a lot of what he said when he started talking about navigational aids and headings and all kinds of things I wasn't familiar with, so I pulled my journal and a pen out of my duffel bag and asked him to repeat it. I could have easily hired another pilot to take me to the island. I could have been on my way there the next morning. I sat on a bench in the airport terminal for almost two hours, trying to decide whether or not to go back." I hesitate because this is the moment I've been dreading. "But I didn't because it suddenly seemed pointless. What good was it if I could find the island, but I couldn't find Calia? So instead of returning to the island, I packed up my stuff and left. Took the first plane out. And that's why I came here. To tell you how much I regret that decision."

Anna looks like she might cry. Or throw up. Or faint. T.J. doesn't look so good either; all the color has drained out of his face. They're probably remembering their first day on the island, and how desperately they wanted to see a plane fly overhead and land in the lagoon. He reaches for Anna's hand. She's not crying, but she has that same look on her face that Calia did when James died: shell-shocked.

I know there's nothing I can say that will change how they feel, so I wait for them to speak.

"You okay, sweetie?" T.J. asks Anna.

She nods her head, takes a deep breath, and lets it out. "I'm okay," she says.

T.J. begins to speak. "Anna and I have this philosophy. She told me once when we were on the island, 'What's done is done.' We'd discovered your shack and the plastic container you used to collect water. If we'd found it earlier, we might not have drunk the pond water, which meant we wouldn't have gotten sick and we would have been on the beach when the rescue plane flew over. There was a second plane that flew over after we'd been on the island for about a year. If it had spotted us, we'd have been rescued earlier and Anna would have been able to spend time with her parents before they passed away. But those things didn't happen. What's done *is* done. We can hardly blame you for a decision that you had no idea would affect us. We still won, Owen. We survived and we have this great life. I understand why you came here and why needed to tell us your story. But you can let it go, okay?"

I don't think I've ever been so overcome by emotion in my life. I can't speak, because I'm in danger of breaking down right in front of them. I nod instead, and look away, taking deep breaths. When I find some measure of control I say, "I'm going back to the island, to do what I promised I would do. Knowing what you've been through, I feel like it's the only way for me to come full circle. I'm not staying long—one night only—but I wondered if you might consider coming along, T.J."

"Is it still there?" T.J. asks. "We thought the island had been decimated during the tsunami."

"It's still there. I hired a pilot who agreed to check it out for me, using the information I'd written down about where it was located."

He doesn't say anything at first, but then he glances at Anna and says, "Thanks. I'm gonna have to pass."

"I understand," I say. "Just thought I'd ask."

A baby's cries fill the room and it startles me because it's so loud. T.J. crosses the room and turns down the baby monitor that's sitting on a side table.

"I'll check on her," Anna says. She walks over to me and gives me a hug. "Good night, Owen. It was so nice to meet you."

It's late, and T.J. walks me to the door. "When are you going?" he asks.

"My flight to Malé is in seven days. Plenty of time if you should change your mind. And the flight and all expenses would be on me."

"It would scare Anna."

"Like I said. I understand completely."

"Are you flying out of O'Hare?" T.J. asks.

"Yes."

"Then come back tomorrow night. Have dinner with us again. I'll invite my friend Ben. I'm sure he'd like to meet you."

"Okay," I say. "I will. Thanks. For everything."

He nods. "Sure. See you tomorrow."

Chapter 15

T.J.

AFTERWARD, WHEN OWEN HAS gone back to his hotel, I walk into the nursery. Anna is sitting in the chair rocking Piper, who is still fussing. "Is it her teeth?" I ask.

Anna nods. "Probably. She's got one ready to poke through. I gave her some Motrin."

I cross the room, bend down near the rocking chair, and stroke the baby's head. "Are you okay?" I ask.

She nods.

"You sure?"

"Yes." She seems fragile, like she might shatter into a million pieces at any moment. But she won't; she's tougher than that.

"That was hard to hear," I say.

"Yes," she says. "It took a lot of courage for him to come here."

I know Anna doesn't blame Owen, and what I told him was true. We've gone down the "if-only" road and we decided a long time ago that there was no sense in dwelling on things we couldn't change. In the grand scheme of things, we consider ourselves lucky. But Anna lost more than I did while we were on the island, and I'd bet money that she's thinking about her parents and how much she misses them right now.

"I know you want to go back to the island with Owen," she says.

I open my mouth to protest, but she shakes her head.

"I know you better than anyone I've ever known. I could see it on your face, T.J."

She's absolutely right.

I do want to go. And this time I want to arrive and leave under my own power, not be plunged into the ocean or blown off the beach. I want to stand on that sand and know that I'm there on my terms. I want to know that while I'm there, Anna and the kids are safe at home, waiting for me.

"Not one thing was by choice when we were there," I say. "I would like to stand on that beach and know that I'm the one who's in control this time."

"You know I would never hold you back from doing something you wanted to do," she says. "I think you should go with Owen."

"You hate that island," I counter.

"I do," she says. "I hate that such a beautiful, breathtaking place almost killed us. But without it I wouldn't have you. And if you want to go back, then go. You have my blessing."

I nod my head, thinking as I often do that she is the most remarkable person I've ever known.

"I'll come to bed in a minute," she says. "I'm going to rock Piper."

Piper has stopped fussing and fallen back to sleep. But I know that it's Anna's way of telling me she needs to be alone with her memories for a little while longer, so I kiss both of them and say, "Okay."

Chapter 16

Owen

I'M SITTING IN ANNA AND T.J.'s living room the next evening when the doorbell rings.

"That's probably Ben," T.J. says. He opens the door and greets his friend, then welcomes him inside.

I rise from my chair and cross the room to where they're standing.

"This is Owen," T.J. says.

Ben takes a step toward me with an outstretched hand. "Hey, I'm Ben. It's nice to meet you. T.J. told me your story. That's wild, man."

"It's nice to meet you, too," I say.

"Uncle Benny," Mick shouts, bursting into the room and barreling toward Ben.

"Hey there, Mickey Mouse." Ben scoops him up and spins him around. "Whatcha been up to, little buddy?" He keeps spinning him, faster and faster, and Mick is laughing so hard he can't answer.

Anna walks by with the baby in her arms. "If he pukes like he did the last time you did that, you're cleaning it up," she says.

They slowly stop spinning and when Ben sets Mick down the little boy immediately falls over.

"Again!" Mick says.

"I can't," Ben says. "If you puke, your mom's gonna get pissed at me. Don't tell her I said *pissed* in front of you, okay?"

"Pissed!" Mick shouts.

Josie walks up to Ben and hands him a plastic teacup. He doesn't miss a beat and pretends to drink it all down. "Thanks, Jos. Can I please have a refill?" She walks away toward her play kitchen, which is set up in a corner of the living room.

Anna walks back into the room. "Dinner's ready. Who wants a taco?"

"Me!" the kids shout, and we follow them into the kitchen.

After dinner, T.J. tells me he'd like to go back to the island with me if the offer still stands.

"Of course," I say. I'm surprised, because I really hadn't expected to hear those words from him. "What made you change your mind?"

"Anna," T.J. says. He looks at her and she smiles back at him, and I get the feeling there's probably more to it than that. T.J. puts his arm around her and she lays her head on his shoulder.

Ben leans toward my chair. "They're always really touchy-feely. You'll get used to it," he says.

T.J. starts laughing. "He's one to talk. If Stacy were here, she'd be in his lap right now, with her tongue in his ear."

"Damn right she would," Ben says. He looks at me. "Stacy's my fiancée. We're getting married in a few months. She wanted to come tonight, but she had some wedding stuff to take care of. That girl has turned into a major bridezilla. But I don't care because I love her."

"Congratulations," I say.

Anna stands up and pushes her chair back. "I'm going to put the kids to bed and then go read in the bedroom. I'll leave you guys to talk."

T.J. also rises. "I'll help you round them up." He stops in front of a cupboard, opens it, and pulls out a bottle of whiskey. "Owen?" he asks.

"Sure," I say.

Anna crosses to the refrigerator. "I bought some beer, Ben."

"I'll just have whiskey," he says.

"Are you sure?" Anna asks. "Because I've got Bud Light." She's smiling and it sounds like she's teasing him. She pulls out a longneck bottle and holds it up. "I picked up some at the store the other day, just for you."

"No, I'm good," he says.

"Stay here, T.J. I can get the kids down." On her way out of the kitchen Anna gives him a lingering kiss. Ben points to his cheek and clears his throat, and she laughs and gives him a quick peck.

"Your wife just kissed me, T.J. You'll probably want to keep a close eye on us."

T.J. gets out three glasses and uncaps the bottle. "I'm not remotely worried," he says with a snort, pouring the whiskey into our glasses.

"That hurts, man," Ben says, laughing. "That really hurts."

"What I want to know," I say two hours later, "is how come my house was a shack, but your house was a house." This question strikes me as slightly funny, but that's probably because the level of whiskey in the bottle is quite a bit lower than it was.

"Don't get me wrong," T.J. says. "Your house was stellar. Really well done. But the heat and humidity are not forgiving when it comes to wood." Or bodies, I might add, but I don't want to bring everyone down. "Some of that wood was pretty rotten." He takes another drink. "It didn't look quite as good as you remember when we found it." He picks up the bottle and pours some more whiskey into my glass. "Why'd you build it in the woods, anyway? Jesus, the rats."

"I thought the trees would give me some protection from the storms—and they did. I always worried that one might fall on the house, though."

"T.J. told me about the big spiders, too," Ben says.

"Brown huntsman," I say. "Creepy as hell."

"Word," T.J. says, leaning over to clink his glass against mine.

"You okay with sleeping on the beach?" I ask, directing my question to T.J.

"Sure. Won't be the first time."

"I'm traveling light. Not planning on bringing a tent. Just a duffel and sleeping bag. Enough food and water for about twenty-four hours. "

"Fine by me. City Boy over there is the one who'd need high-end camping gear," T.J. says. "He works in a bank. Wears a tie every day. Drinks *lattes*."

"I love my job—and lattes—so you can fuck off, Callahan," Ben says. But he smiles at T.J., and I can tell by his tone that he's kidding. Good for him. Steady job, girl he loves. What more could you want?

"Why don't you come with us?" I ask.

"Me?" Ben says.

He probably thinks it's the whiskey talking, but I'm sincere. "Sure," I say. "Do you have a passport?"

"Yeah," Ben says.

"Can you get the time off?"

"I've got some vacation days I might not have mentioned to Stacy, but only because I was afraid she'd make me use them for some weird wedding shit that I don't need to be a part of."

"T.J.?"

"It would be great if Ben came along," he says.

"Okay, then. It's settled," Ben says. "Stacy's probably gonna blow a gasket, but she'll come around."

"Cheers," I say, and we raise our glasses.

"What are we toasting to?" Ben asks.

"Returning home safely," T.J. says, and the three of us down our drinks.

Chapter 17

T.J.

I TELL BEN TO CRASH in the den and give Owen the couch in the living room. No one's really hammered, but no one should be driving, either. I turn off lights and lock up, then head down the hallway. Josie is asleep on her back, clutching her favorite blanket. I tuck the covers in around her and go to Mick's room. He wakes up when I put his teddy bear back in his arms. Groggy, he looks at me and says, "Can I have some water, Daddy?"

I walk to the kitchen and fill a sippy cup with water. When I hand it to him he takes a few sips and falls right back to sleep. Piper is sleeping on her stomach, with her little diapered butt sticking up in the air. I cover her, too, even though it will do no good. She'll just kick her blanket off again.

After I check on the kids I walk into the bedroom, very happy to see that Anna is still awake. I lock the door behind me.

She's lying on top of the covers, propped up by a couple of pillows, and all she's wearing is a tank top with thin straps and a tiny pair of black underwear. She marks her page and then set her book on the nightstand, giving me a smile.

I strip off my clothes—all of them—and join her on the bed.

"You taste like whiskey," she says when I pull her into my arms and kiss her. She runs her hands across my chest, letting them drift lower, which makes me happier still. "I like the way you taste. Kiss me again."

So I do. I also remove her tank top and run my fingers lightly over her skin. She lets out a soft sigh. She's always beautiful to me, but she looks especially beautiful right now, because I can see and feel and hear what my touch is doing to her.

"I need you," I say.

"I'm yours."

I know she's often tired, and that chasing after three kids wears her out, but very rarely does she tell me no. She still worries about the cancer coming back, and she told me once that she considers it a gift every time we make love. I do, too. But not because there's anything to worry about with my health. It's because she chose this life with me, and I know how very lucky I am.

I take off her underwear, sliding them down slowly, and start to touch her. She moans and tells me it feels good, tells me not to stop. I love the way she gives herself to me completely, how she never holds back.

"Now," she says, pulling me up so that I can slide inside of her. It feels every bit as good as it always does and it doesn't take long before I'm the one whispering in her ear, moaning, telling her that I love her.

I'm close, but I wait until she clenches around me and then I don't hold back. She holds on to me tightly and says my name over and over as our breathing and our movement slows.

I could listen to her say it forever and it still wouldn't be long enough.

Chapter 18

T.J.

ON THE DAY WE LEAVE for the Maldives, Stacy and Anna go with us to O'Hare. We drop the kids off at my parents' house and after assuring my mom repeatedly that nothing will go wrong, and that I'll be home before they know it, we get back in the car.

Stacy's uncharacteristically quiet, which Ben whispers is a bad sign. "It actually means she's about to come unglued," he says, so he's doing his best to calm her down. "It's okay, Stace," I hear him say. "It'll be fine. Don't worry. I mean, seriously, what are the odds?"

Anna sits in the passenger seat and she's a bit quiet, too.

"You're not worried are you?" I ask.

"Maybe a little."

"You know we've taken every precaution."

"I know you have."

Before we go through security I kiss her good-bye. "I love you. I'll miss you and the kids. And I'll be back soon."

She kisses me back with everything she has. "Anything less isn't an option, T.J."

Ben and Stacy are locked in an embrace, like they're afraid they'll never see each other again. Owen and I wait patiently until I remind Ben that if he doesn't wrap it up soon, he's going to make us all late. Anna peels Stacy off of him, suggesting they go out for coffee, and the three of us finally head for security.

It's the same route Anna and I flew when I was sixteen years old: Chicago to Germany and Germany to Sri Lanka and then finally to Malé. It's been more than ten years, but in some ways it feels like yesterday. The trip goes off without a hitch this time, though, and I tell myself it's a good sign.

When we land in the Maldives and walk outside to catch the shuttle to the seaplane terminal, the heat brings back strong memories. The hot humid air presses down on me, and feels slightly suffocating.

"Jesus, it's hot. I think even my hair is sweating," Ben says.

"It probably is," I say.

The seaplane pilot looks like the polar opposite of Mick Forrester. Captain Harrison Bradley is young and fit and tells us he's from Canada. I glance down. He's also wearing shoes.

We board the seaplane and buckle in. It's not like I have trouble flying, and Anna and I have been on planes together several times since we flew on that chartered Learjet that brought us home after being rescued, but there's a slight feeling of unease that I can't quite shake as we fly over the open water.

When the pilot alerts us that we're approaching the island I stare out my window. The aerial view of the island mesmerizes me because it's weird to see it from above. It's weird to be seeing it at all.

Landing feels surreal to me, and probably Ben, too, but for completely different reasons. Neither of us have ever been on a plane that landed in a lagoon; it's quite different from crashing into the ocean. There's no dock, so we jump from the plane right into the shallow water, our bags slung over our shoulders.

In addition to our sleeping bags and duffels, we've each got several large bottles of water, some nonperishable food, and our cell phones. Captain Bradley told us that, due to advances in technology, most notably cell towers, our cell phones will probably still work. I turn mine on and exhale when I see that the signal is nice and strong.

"I'll be back in the morning," Captain Bradley says. "I can't fly in the dark, but you'll be fine overnight. I know exactly where you are."

We thank him and he wades back into the water, walking toward the seaplane.

I remember what I said to Anna when I told her why I wanted to come back here. How I wanted to stand on the beach and feel like I was in control.

But I don't feel like I'm in control at all.

I feel like the only reason I'm alive to stand on this beach again is because of luck, or fate, or whatever you want to call it. I don't feel invincible. I feel vulnerable, powerless. My heartbeat hammers in my chest and I swallow hard. I've never had a panic attack in my life, but I worry that I may be about to experience my first.

"You okay, man?" Ben asks.

I don't want Owen and Ben to think I can't handle this, although I'm not sure I actually can. So I take a few deep breaths and get my shit together fast. I think of Anna, healthy and happy. The kids. Our home. All of it ours.

"Yeah. I'm okay," I say. "Let's do this."

Owen turns around and gives a signal to the pilot and my heartbeat stutters once more when I watch the seaplane lift off and fly away.

We walk the beach first. It looks so familiar. Same shoreline. Same clear blue water. Same danger if you're not careful. I stand there, white sand under my feet, and feel the breeze coming off the ocean. Owen points to the reef. "Way out there is where I saw the whale shark. That's all James was trying to do the day he died. See if he could spot one, too."

After the beach we head inland. It's just as buggy and damp as I remember. There's no trace of either of our houses, but we show Ben the general location where Owen built his. It's hard to be exact because the island's vegetation seems to be thicker than ever.

It takes us a half hour to find the cave. It shouldn't be that hard to find, but the opening is really blocked this time and it takes some digging to clear the plant debris away. "Is this it?"

Ben asks.

Owen nods. "Yeah."

"Is he still in there?" I ask.

On the flight over, Owen mentioned that he was worried about the tsunami displacing the body. Maybe the water had filled the cave and when it receded it took the bones with it.

"Only one way to find out," he says.

Owen has brought a small flashlight and he pulls it from his pocket and lies down on the ground, inching forward. He keeps going until the only thing sticking out of the cave are his shoes.

"Well?" I shout.

I get my answer when he wriggles out and places the skull on the ground at my feet. I crouch, remembering the day when I first found it. How I wondered who it belonged to. What had happened to him or her.

Owen stands up, brushes the dirt from his hands, and wipes his face with his forearm. "It looks like all the bones are still there. I'll get my bag."

Ben and I help Owen retrieve the bones from the cave. At one point, the three of us are stuffed into the opening of the cave side by side. Ben holds the flashlight while Owen and I feel around, making sure we aren't leaving any part of the skeleton behind.

We place the bones in the extra-large duffel bag Owen brought. "What now?" I ask. "You can't bring a skeleton on a commercial flight, can you?"

Owen shakes his head. "The remains will be shipped by the local funeral home in Malé; I've already been in contact with them to arrange it. Captain Bradley has agreed to transport the bones to the mainland for me."

I clap Owen on the back. "It's over. You did what you came to do."

When the sun goes down I tell Ben to watch the sky. "Why?" he asks.

"You'll see." It isn't long before Ben does see, because the bats fill the sky, blocking out the light of the moon.

"Holy shitballs," he says. "There must be hundreds, maybe thousands. Where do they go during the day?"

"I don't know," I say. "I don't think I want to know."

We build a roaring fire on the beach, and eat the food we brought with us: chips and beef jerky and crackers and peanut butter sandwiches.

"Why haven't you come for the bones before now?" Ben asks.

"I'd somewhat made peace with the fact that this would be James's final resting place. Kind of like those climbers that die on Mount Everest. It would be better to bring the bodies down, but they're not easy to get to and people treat them with respect, so they stay. I don't have regular Internet access—I've been offline for years and I don't really miss it—but a few months ago I had the opportunity to use a computer. I Googled the Maldives on a whim, really. I'd spent enough time here that I was just curious. Thought I'd see what was going on. I never expected to discover the things I did. I read about T.J. and Anna, and what had happened to them. I read all the news stories, going back through pages and pages of coverage about the crash and the rescue. One of the links led me to a news story that mentioned the skeleton they'd found, and how they'd told the police about it after their rescue. I knew James's resting place was no longer as secure as I thought it would be. If Anna and T.J. could find him, there was a chance someone else might, too, someday. So here we are."

None of us says anything for a while. We stare at the fire and I listen to the crash of the waves. "Whatever happened to those business partners of yours, Owen?" I ask.

"I looked them up, too. They had one of the largest IPOs in the country. But they never delivered on their product or earned enough income to offset their spending. When the bubble burst their stock price tanked and was only worth pennies on the dollar. They went bankrupt in early 2001."

"Wow," I say. "Guess you called that one."

"I guess so," he says.

Later, when Owen has fallen asleep, Ben turns to me and says, "Is it hard for you? Being here?"

I've been lying here unable to sleep, mentally counting down the minutes until the seaplane will return, trying to make sense of it all. "I've got all these memories, Ben. All these sights and sounds and smells flooding my system, and none of them feel good. I thought I would feel invincible if I came back here, but I don't. I still feel powerless. I want to go home, back to Anna and the kids."

"I get that," he says. "But whether you agree with me or not, you kicked this island's ass, T.J. There aren't very many people in the world who could make it through something like this."

"You'd be surprised what people can do when they have no other choice, Ben."

"Maybe so. But I'm not best friends with any of them."

"Thanks for coming with me," I say.

"Anytime."

In the morning, I use my phone to take pictures so I can show Anna and my parents what I've seen, what the island looks like now. The pictures will show a place that's breathtakingly beautiful, yet beautifully deceiving.

And when the seaplane lands in the lagoon, I'm the first one on it.

Chapter 19

Owen

I PACK UP MY THINGS and walk outside. We got home from the Maldives late yesterday, and T.J. and I both slept clear through to the next morning. Now, I've got another plane to catch in about three hours.

Anna is sitting on the steps blowing bubbles, with Piper on her lap. The baby seems to love this, and she reaches out a tiny hand, trying to pop them.

"Feel rested?" she asks.

"Getting there," I say. "Do you know where T.J. is?"

"He and the twins are over there," she says, pointing to a wooden structure that runs alongside the garage.

"What is that?" I ask.

She smiles. "It's a chicken coop. We have five of them. They make great pets." She blows another round of bubbles and Piper laughs. I watch as T.J. comes around the corner, Josie and Mick holding on to his hands.

"I was thinking about Calia while you were gone," Anna says. "Whatever happened to her, Owen? Why didn't she call?"

I sit down on the steps beside her. "After your seaplane went down I was in a pretty bad place. I went home. Made peace with my family. My sister had divorced her loser husband by then, but my mom was still with my stepdad. He'd finally gotten his shit together a little and she seemed happy. I hung around, trying to think of what I wanted to do next. But then I realized how stupid I was being. I had the financial resources and I definitely had the time. So why the hell wasn't I looking for her? I started by flying to Farnham. It wasn't that difficult to track down her address. I expected her to swing open the door and then I'd demand that she tell me why she never called. But no one answered when I rang the bell, and I was really disappointed because she should have been back by then. But small towns have one major thing going for them: Everyone knows your business. Calia's neighbor was outside watering flowers when I arrived, and she was happy to tell me all about Calia, and where I could find her, which turned out to be a small, remote village in Africa. By the way, Africa is a really big place."

Anna laughs. "It isn't exactly small."

"It took me a while to track her down. It turned out that she'd signed up for another volunteer project, and the organization she was with was not real eager to divulge the location of their volunteers, understandably. I persisted but kept running into one dead end after another. Finally, I got lucky and one day, after weeks of searching, I walked into a village and started looking around for girls with long blond hair. When I spotted her, in the middle of a group of African children, I remember being the happiest I'd been in a long time. I didn't even care if she minded that I'd tracked her down. I was just glad I'd found her."

"What did she say?" Anna leans forward, as if she's eager to hear my response.

"She threw herself into my arms, crying, and said, 'I hope you are here to un-break my heart, Owen. I've been waiting so long for you to come and find me.'"

"Why didn't you call?" I'd asked.

"Because my purse was stolen on the way home. My phone was inside it. I had no way to find *you*," she said.

"Then what happened?"

"Then I kissed her like my life depended on it."

"Oh, Owen," Anna says. She has tears in her eyes.

"It made sense then. I hadn't been wrong about her feelings for me."

"Where is she now? Is she still in Africa?"

"Yes. We both live in that village, as volunteers. It makes her happy. And she's my wife now, which makes *me* happy. It was hard for me to tell her that James's body had been discovered. When I finally tracked her down in Africa the first thing I told her was that I hadn't gone back to get him like I said I would. I felt horrible about that, and I was sure she'd break down. Tell me how disappointed she was in me. I don't know if it was because enough time had gone by, but she said it was okay, that she'd made her peace with it, just like I had. She had lots of ways to remember him—pictures and his personal items, many of which she kept. But we both knew it was time to bring James back. She didn't want to come with me. She has a lot of... bad memories. She said, 'I will be waiting in Farnham to welcome him home, Owen.'"

"What did you whisper in her ear?" Anna asks. "When you put her on the plane to go home? What did you say to her?"

"I told her I loved her."

"And what did she say?"

"She said, 'I love you, too.'"

Anna wipes her eyes. "That's beautiful , Owen."

T.J. walks up to us, the twins following closely behind. He kneels down beside Anna, a concerned expression on his face. "Why are you crying?" he asks.

"Don't worry," she says. "They're happy tears. There's nothing I love more than a good happy ending."

Epilogue

Owen

Six months later

I HOLD CALIA'S LEFT HAND and she carries the flowers in her right. Daisies this time. It's always different. She chooses whatever catches her eye. Three-year-old Adhra skips along ahead of us, singing softly to herself. Before Adhra came to the orphanage, she lived in the slums of Kenya, foraging for food after her parents died. She came home with us three months ago, and I can't imagine her ever leaving our sides.

The cemetery is old and quaint, with cobblestone paths and crumbling tombstones, some of them dating back a hundred years or more. It's where Calia's mother, Eleanor, is buried, and we stop there first. Calia hands half of the flowers to Adhra and lets her put them in the little metal vase beside the headstone. This is Adhra's job, and we would never think of taking it away from her. She gets immeasurable joy from such small things.

The next grave we visit is newer. The headstone reads JAMES COLIN REED, BELOVED BROTHER AND SON. Knowing her brother is home gives Calia immeasurable comfort. As for me, I can almost visit James's grave without guilt and remorse. Almost, but not quite.

Once the flowers have been placed we linger for a few minutes.

"I'm ready now," Calia says. She takes Adhra's hand and we turn to go.

We're going to be here for a while, in Farnham. We live in Calia's childhood home because that's what she wants and I would find it nearly impossible to deny her something that makes her so happy. Besides, it was my desire to finally put down roots, to stop going wherever it was that we were needed. Not because I wanted to stop helping, but because I have a family of my own to take care of. And right now Calia and I are working on trying to expand our family to give Adhra a brother or sister. I'd hardly call it work, though, considering what's involved. We'll raise our family, not on the arid plains of Kenya, but here. Where Calia grew up. This house can hold a family of four with ease, but if we ever grow out of it, maybe Calia will finally allow me to buy her a bigger one.

After I drive us home I park the car and then pick up Adhra and settle her on my shoulders for the short walk to our front door. She giggles and pulls my hair, but I don't scold her. It's a small price to pay to hear her laugh.

"Someone needs a haircut," Calia says. "You've simply got too much. It's hard for her to resist."

I lean over and kiss her. "You know what? I think you're hard to resist."

"You're very lucky then. Because I happen to find you irresistible as well."

"I'm so glad we got that out of the way, Calia."

She laughs and follows me into the house. "Me, too, Owen. Me, too."

ACKNOWLEDGMENTS

To my editor, Jill Schwartzman: Thank you for suggesting the e-Special. I always wondered what happened to the guy who built the shack. Now I know (and so will everyone else).

To my publicist, Amanda Walker: Thank you for everything you do to make my life easier. I couldn't do this without you.

To Jane Dystal, Miriam Goderich, and Lauren Abramo: Thank you for being the best agents a writer could ever hope for.

To the entire team at Penguin Dutton and Plume: Thank you for being a publisher who goes above and beyond in everything you do. I couldn't be in better hands.

Thank you to Kent Lewis for answering my many questions about airplanes and navigation. You're one of the nicest men I know.

Thank you to Andrew McAllister for answering my questions about storing computer data and also for sharing my love of Stephen King's *The Stand*.

Special thanks to Dallal BenRomdhane for being British and living in the Maldives . Two birds, one stone, my dear. You answered all my questions about the Maldives (and sent pictures!), and when I first heard Calia's voice in my head she clearly had an English accent.

To my beta readers Laura Bradley Rede, Catherine McKenzie, and Peggy Hildebrandt: Thank you for your willingness to look at this manuscript on such short notice, and also your valuable feedback. I appreciate it so much.

A heartfelt shout-out to the bloggers who champion my books every single day: Autumn Hull, Andrea Pierce Thompson, April Haug, Asheley Tart, Jaime Arkin, Erin Arkin, Jenny Aspinall, Gitte Doherty, Wanda Morales, Denise Tung, Nicola Farrell, Natasha Tomic, Madison Seidler, Chandra Haun, Mandy Iread-indie, NedaAmini, Amy Lazarus Bromberg, Melissa Amster, Stephanie Elliot, Liz Clark Fenton and Lisa Steinke Dannenfeldt of Chick Lit Is Not Dead, Tina's Book Reviews, Rosette Alcantara Doyle, Gina Halsted Brown, Aestas BookBlogger, Christine Bezdenejnih Estevez, Jana Waterreus, Racquel at The Book Barbie, Amy at Book Loving Mom, and Yara Santos.

And last but certainly not least, thank you once again to my devoted readers. None of this would be possible without you.

ABOUT THE AUTHOR

Tracey Garvis Graves is a *New York Times, Wall Street Journal,* and *USA Today* bestselling author. Her debut novel, *On the Island,* spent 9 weeks on the *New York Times* bestseller list, has been translated into twenty-seven languages, and is in development with MGM and Temple Hill Productions for a feature film. In addition to *On the Island* and *Uncharted,* she is also the author of *Covet, Every Time I Think of You,* and *Cherish.* She can be found on Facebook at www.facebook.com/tgarvisgraves and Twitter at https://twitter.com/tgarvisgraves or you can visit her website at http://traceygarvisgraves.com

Made in the USA
San Bernardino, CA
23 January 2016